The explosion shook the earth as the plane burst into flames.

My heart was racing and my breath was coming too fast.

"It's okay," he said.

I could feel the heat coming off the burning wreckage. I couldn't catch my breath.

He placed his palm on my chest beneath my neck. "It's okay," he said, again, shifting so that all I saw was his gaze on mine.

"Breathe with me," he said, taking a long slow breath.

I did. I stumbled with it at first, but then I mirrored his breathing and felt a little more in control.

"I need to get you back to my cabin," he said, lightly touching my forehead. "You bumped your head. I need to get you cleaned up so you can rest."

"The ringing…" I said.

"That's normal," he said. "It'll go away. Can you stand?"

I held onto his arms as he pulled me to me feet. My legs felt weak and I didn't trust them to hold me. I held onto his arms so tight, my nails dug into his skin.

Seeming to know this, to understand, he bent down and swooped me up into his arms again.

He was strong and seemed to have no trouble whatsoever carrying me. I leaned my cheek against his chest and closed my eyes.

Safe. I was safe now.

BILLIONAIRE FALLEN ANGEL

ALSO BY KATHRYN KALEIGH

THE WORTHINGTONS

BILLIONAIRE FALLEN ANGEL

THE WORTHINGTONS

KATHRYN KALEIGH

To learn more about Kathryn Kaleigh, visit

www.kathrynkaleigh.com

Kathryn Kaleigh

1

CAMILA WORTHINGTON

"Mayday. Mayday. Mayday."

A night flight. I never did night flights. Well sometimes. But never in the mountains.

It was a clear night. About as clear as anyone could ask for.

I could see the mountain peaks sprawled out below me, so running into the side of a mountain wasn't a concern. Shouldn't be anyway.

But the plane *felt...* off.

No one responded to my premature distress call. Pressing my hands against the rich leather wheel, I took a deep breath. Let it out slowly.

Everything was okay. It was a good thing no one had responded. It would be hard to explain *feeling off* to those who worked with machines.

I was thirty minutes away from the little Whiskey Springs airport. Runway. It was Whiskey Springs runway. It didn't even have a terminal, so I dubbed it a runway. Not an airport.

The big gangly lab with solid black fur sitting in the passenger seat next to me let out a little whimper.

"It's okay, Biscuit. I'll have you on the ground in no time at all. Your new owner is waiting for you."

Biscuit barked one time.

"You a nervous flyer?" I asked with a quick glance over at the dog. He just blinked at me. "No need to worry."

"No need to worry," I repeated, this time to myself, straightening in my seat.

It was just me and Biscuit, the airplane, and the night sky.

Biscuit was a trained, certified seeing-eye dog on his way to his new owner. A fifteen-year-old girl who had been in an accident, leaving her totally blind.

I could have… should have… waited until after the storm to get Biscuit to his new owner, but I wanted to get him to the girl as soon as possible. *Before the storm.* Once these mountain storms set in, they could last for days.

I suppose I took after my Aunt Ainsley. She had created a whole company around delivering pets for those who needed them. *Pilots for Pets.* A division of my grandfather's company, Pilots for Pets was devoted to flying pets anywhere in the country they needed to go.

I worked for her. And it was shocking how many pets needed to be flown somewhere every day.

Sometimes she flew regular, non-certified pets for people to adopt. An animal lover, she believed that she was making a difference. And I was right there with her.

Static came through the radio. Flying tonight had not been my best decision. But Biscuit needed to be with his new owner. Amy. Her name was Amy.

I tried again, minus the distress call. "This is Flight 555. Just checking in. Anybody listening?"

No response. Just the steady roar of the jet's engines. Typically I loved being in the air. Alone. It was considered by a lot of people, namely the psychologists in my family, to be a form of meditation. I did not doubt it. A couple of days without flying and I started to get antsy.

My Aunt Brianna believed that all pilots were addicted to the quiet, peacefulness of being literally on top of the world.

But tonight there was no time for relaxation. Tonight I had to be alert and watch not just the computers, but keep my eyes on the visual, too.

Ainsley usually took the western flights. I tended to stay south. But she had a thing this weekend with her husband. And me, being newly piloted and single, volunteered for anything and everything that had to do with flying.

It wasn't my fault. Love of aviation ran through my veins. My grandfather Noah Worthington had started a private charter company with just one airplane. Then he added another. And another.

His company exploded. The doubters said he was growing too fast. But he handled it like a natural. Grew it smoothly into an empire. And now... Now he owned hundreds of planes based around the country.

When pilots graduated with their aviation degrees, they vied to work for Noah Worthington. The big airlines were no longer the name of the game.

My grandfather, Noah Worthington was. And my father, Quinn Worthington ran the whole thing now. Daddy had never flown a plane in his life, but had taken what Grandpa had started and grew it into a gigantic family business.

The plane shifted.

I was almost to the airport, just minutes out. I was in the correct position.

The directional dial made a little flip, then settled back with a wobble. The plane went into a descent I had not authorized.

A microburst?

Altitude warning alarms began beeping.

I gave the plane full power, but the descent continued.

Forcing myself to stay calm, I went to the next step.

Lowered the landing gear.

I wasn't going to make the airport runway at this rate.

I pulled out of the dive with full power.

"Something's wrong with the system," I muttered. "We're going to stall."

Biscuit whimpered and, lowering his head, covered his eyes with his paws.

"Agreed," I said and started a controlled descent.

But I was too high.

I switched off the motor.

A bold move. But I could recover.

My heart pounded hard against my chest.

Then we began to level off and the warning alarms stopped.

I blew out a breath. Biscuit peeked out at me with one eye.

"We're okay," I said. Biscuit uncovered his face and sat up.

If he wasn't a smart dog, I didn't know what one was.

My heart rate returned to normal. I checked all my systems. Everything was back on track for landing at Whiskey Springs.

I looked down, out the window, watching for any indication of the airport. How was I supposed to find an unlit runway in the dark?

Should have thought of that.

Then everything started beeping again. All the warning alarms were going off. Deafeningly loud now.

I was losing altitude.

I could not see the runway ahead. Just mountains and valleys covered with trees. And snow. Trees and snow. No airport in sight. Nothing that resembled a runway.

Just alarms going off. Screens flashing.

"Mayday. Mayday. Mayday." I barely recognized my own voice. But I was trained for this. Right?

I checked the locator signal. Sent a distress alert. Nothing happened.

Nothing was working.

System failure.

We were going fast. Much too fast. Nothing was correcting.

I braced myself.

We were going to crash.

The moon had gone behind the clouds or a mountain or somewhere. It was pitch dark now. I couldn't see a thing.

The plane was shaking now. We were going down. Not a nosedive. But a quick level descent. Not that it mattered in these mountains. A level descent could be straight into the side of a snow-capped mountain.

I gripped the wheel and held on to it for dear life and closed my eyes.

So many thoughts crossed through my mind.

Trying to focus, I could not help but wonder if my twin brother knew I was in trouble. Would he sense it?

Biscuit whimpered.

I reached out and gripped his paw.

"We're going to be okay," I told the dog.

Then I prayed. *Please let me be right.*

"Mayday. Mayday! Mayday!!"

2

BEAU MONTROSE

I wanted nothing more than to be left alone.

That was the whole purpose of renting a cabin in the mountains for three months. Longer if I wanted.

I heated a bag of popcorn in the microwave, poured it into a bowl, and went to sit in front of the fireplace.

No television. No Internet. No phone service.

I was here to think. To reset.

To figure out what it was I wanted to do next.

I was thirty-three years old. Four years of Air Force. ROTC. Eleven—three weeks shy of twelve—years committed to the Air Force.

My whole life had been wrapped around the military. My father before me and my grandfather before him. My great-grandfather had fought in World War II.

I came from a long line of men who had fought and died for their country.

When I'd enlisted, I figured I'd die in the service. Just like my father and his father and his father.

It was what the men in my family did. They got married. Had a son. Then went to war and died.

I knew where I went wrong. I had enlisted without getting married and without having a son. So I'd broken the streak.

As a result... maybe not connected... but still possible... the military had kicked me to the curb. Honorable discharge. Full retirement. All that. But new President. New rules. The military was too big.

So now it wasn't. And hundreds, maybe thousands of us were dumped out as over-trained, warped civilians.

And now all my plans had gone up in flames just like the logs in the fireplace.

I leaned back in my chair and closed my eyes. I was trained to always be on alert. I doubted that instinct would ever go away.

It hadn't exactly been purposeful, my breaking of the family destiny. But it seemed admirable to not leave a widow alone to fend for herself and her children.

My mother had done her duty. She had raised me up. Sent me to college. Then she had

done the unthinkable. She had remarried and moved off to God only knew where with her new husband. We didn't keep in touch. Last I heard from social media, she was in Italy.

She had asked me not to join the military. I'd insisted. And it had gone downhill from there. How could she not understand tradition?

As far as me getting married, I figured I would meet someone while I was active duty. Someone who was strong enough to carry on the Montrose family tradition. Alone.

I tossed a piece of kindling into the fireplace. Watched it immediately go up in flames.

Just like my military career.

I had no contingency plan for taking on a second career as a civilian.

A wolf howled in the distance. Less than a minute later, another wolf answered. Water roared as it crashed over the boulders in the shallow river. There was a waterfall not half a mile from here. When the air was super still, I could hear the water crashing over the side of the mountain onto the rocks below.

What I didn't hear was just as important. I didn't hear sounds of civilization. No loud motors. No loud music. No people.

People would just interfere with my thinking.

I finished off my bag of popcorn and contemplated getting another. Instead, I opened another bottle of water and drank it down.

I had nothing against alcohol, but it would just dull my thoughts. And since I was here to think, that made no sense to me.

So I sat and stared into the roaring fire.

There was a storm coming in. Probably sometime in the night. I would wake to a world covered in white, fluffy snow.

Suited me just fine.

I'd take a walk. Follow the river. Enjoy the solitude.

I'd been here for six days and so far all I'd done was to work off some of the mad by chopping enough firewood to last two winters.

When I got the discharge letter, I had been stunned. I'd stayed stunned long enough to get out and get myself here. Then the mad had hit me like a load of bricks.

I decided I would hike out tomorrow and pay Mrs. Dawson for the rest of the winter. It would be nice to be snowed in until spring.

I had electricity out here so it wasn't like it would be a hardship. And I had my computer if I found myself so inclined to write my memoirs or some such. I also had a stack of novels by my favorite authors I'd brought with me.

Yes. I would stay here through the winter. Mrs. Dawson had

warned me that if I was still here when the first big storm came through, I'd probably be here for the duration.

I'd promised to let her know what I decided.

"If I don't hear from you," she'd said. "I'll assume you decided to stay and you can pay up in the spring."

Very kind of her, but I didn't like owing anyone. Besides, I could use some more supplies while I was in town. Some more coke and popcorn. Maybe some frozen pizzas. There was a little store not far down from Mrs. Dawson's house. That's what I would do.

I let my mind go blank as I stared at the crackling fire. It was best to clear out the cobwebs. Dust away the old and start fresh.

At first I thought I imagined it.

Thought I was having a flashback.

Had to be a flashback, I reasoned.

There were no airplanes out here.

Something else I had to work through. They wanted me to go to group therapy. Not happening. I could take a winter and work it out myself. That's what all the old guys did. They didn't sit around in a circle and talk. They worked it out themselves.

That's what I was going to do. Work it out myself.

That's what part of the thinking was all about.

But the roar was getting louder.

This was not a flashback.

I got up and went to the door of my cabin.

I saw nothing, of course, in the darkness.

Just the glow of the moonlight reflecting off a distant mountainside.

I *felt* the airplane as it flew low over my cabin.

Then I felt the air shake as it slammed against the ground.

If I had to bet. No one was walking out of that crash alive.

But no point in betting against myself.

I grabbed my coat and two big flashlights, and took off toward the sound of the crash.

I hadn't gotten far when a gangly black dog met me coming from the plane crash.

He sat down on his haunches. Barked once, then got up and headed back the way he had come.

He wanted me to follow him.

The dog was like Lassie.

And he led me right to the sight of the crash. I used both my flashlights, military grade, to quickly cover the distance.

If I had bet on myself, I would have lost.

Not only had the dog survived, but there was a girl sitting on the ground staring blankly at nothing.

Pieces of what was left of the airplane was behind her.

As I neared her, I could see that she was wearing a uniform.

She looked up at me with big dazed eyes.

"Are you okay?" I asked.

She nodded. "Yes." Then shook her head. "No." She took a deep breath like she had been holding her breath. "Maybe. I don't know."

"Can you stand?" I asked.

"I don't know."

I held out a hand, but she just lowered her head, burying it against the dog's fur.

3

CAMILA

*M*y ears were ringing and I was in a daze.

The dog had barked at me until I had come to and crawled out of the airplane into the darkness.

In the pitch dark, I smelled jet fuel and heat. Tasted something metallic in my mouth. My forehead was damp and sticky with what I had a sick feeling was blood. My blood.

The dog had run off, but he was back now. With someone in tow. Someone with flashlights.

The man spoke to me. Asked if I was okay.

I did not know how to answer him.

"Is there anyone else?" he asked.

He kept asking me questions. I could barely hear him. Could barely think.

When the dog sat down beside me, I wrapped my arms around his neck and buried my face in his fur. He was vaguely familiar. Enough so that I found comfort in him.

The man left for a minute… a few minutes… I don't know how long. Then he came back and knelt next to me.

"Where is the pilot?" he asked. His voice was gentle now. Maybe the ringing in my ears was not quite so bad as it was.

I shook my head. The dog licked my face.

"Is anything broken?" the man asked.

Broken. Was it? I did a mental check of my arms and feet. I felt like hell, but I didn't think anything was broken. I shook my head. "I don't think so."

"Good," he said. "Do you mind if I check? Just to be sure?"

I released my hold on the dog and shook my head again. The man set the flashlights on the ground on either side of me and started with my right hand, gently touching each of my fingers.

He spoke gently as he went. I tried to pay attention, but I only caught parts of what he was saying.

"I'm trained as a field paramedic," he said, moving his hands up my arm to my shoulders and down to my other hand.

Then he checked my ankles and moved up each leg. He moved quickly and competently. It was clear that he was practiced at this.

"Do you know where the pilot is?" he asked again as he put a hand beneath my chin and looked into my eyes.

Pilot? I glanced over at the wreckage of what had once been an airplane. I had been in a crash.

An image of the flashing screens and system alarms going off in the cockpit flashed in my head, but I quickly buried them away.

The dog barked once.

"Is this your dog?"

I glanced over at the gangly black lab sitting protectively next to me.

"Yes," I said. But the startling truth was I honestly did not know. I felt like the world was swirling around me and I couldn't get my footing.

"What's your name?" he asked, ripping off the hem of his shirt and wrapping it around my head. His touch was gentle, but confident.

I did not know this man. But I trusted him.

My name. I wanted to answer. My thoughts were too scattered. I couldn't focus enough to think.

"I don't know." I looked at the man now, searching for something that I could lock onto.

His eyes were kind in a handsome face. He had not shaven for a couple of days, but handsome nonetheless.

But I still did not know him.

I jumped when a piece of metal fell in the plane wreckage.

"We need to move," he said. Without waiting another second, he swooped me up and carried me several yards away from the plane, the dog at our heels.

The explosion shook the earth as the plane burst into flames.

My heart was racing and my breath was coming too fast.

"It's okay," he said.

I could feel the heat coming off the burning wreckage. I couldn't catch my breath.

He placed his palm on my chest beneath my neck. "It's okay," he said, again, shifting so that all I saw was his gaze on mine.

"Breathe with me," he said, taking a long slow breath.

I did. I stumbled with it at first, but then I mirrored his breathing and felt a little more in control.

"I need to get you back to my cabin," he said, lightly touching my forehead. "You bumped your head. I need to get you cleaned up so you can rest."

"The ringing…" I said.

"That's normal," he said. "It'll go away. Can you stand?"

I held onto his arms as he pulled me to me feet. My legs felt weak and I didn't trust them to hold me. I held onto his arms so tight, my nails dug into his skin.

Seeming to know this, to understand, he bent down and swooped me up into his arms again.

He was strong and seemed to have no trouble whatsoever carrying me. I leaned my cheek against his chest and closed my eyes.

Safe. I was safe now.

4

BEAU

*W*hen the plane had gone down, my training had kicked in.

Air Force pararescue. The training had been indelible. For life. That's what they said. And I believed them. If I'd had any doubts, I didn't have them now.

But then the military no longer needed so many of us.

I would find something else to do.

But right now, I had a girl, mid-twenties, head injury following a plane crash.

And suddenly being out here off the grid was not such a good thing. I had no way to call for help.

Holding a flashlight in one hand, the other flashlight tucked in my back pocket, I carried the girl. She was in no shape to walk. The big gangly black lab followed along beside us, taking every step I took with admirable precision. He could be military, he was so precise.

He watched everything I did with this girl and I had little doubt that he would tear into me if I did something to harm her.

As we followed the edge of the river, the first white fluffy snowflakes of the storm began to fall. The storm was coming in sooner than they had predicted. I was predicting a bad one, too.

I got the girl back to my cabin without incident and laid her on my bed. The dog climbed in and laid down beside her.

I turned on the hot water, letting it warm as it ran out of the faucet, but decided the tea kettle would be hotter.

As I filled the tea kettle, I watched the snowflakes drifting down in the moonlight. So pretty when they first started falling. But then when there were too many of them together, they became deadly.

I put the kettle over the gas flame and while I waited for the water to heat, I gathered up a bowl and some washcloths. I put them on the nightstand shoving aside the science fiction book I'd just started reading and pulled up a chair.

The girl's eyes were closed and I could not tell if she was sleeping or unconscious. Either way, she needed to rest.

She had classic features. A heart shaped face. Long, lush eyelashes and bow shaped lips. Her long lush brunette hair had come undone and flowed around her. I swept a strand off her face.

The tea kettle went off, jarring out of my perusal.

I poured hot water into the bowl and after removing the bandage I had made from my shirt, I gently wiped the blood off her forehead. The surface wound did not look too bad, but I had no way of knowing how bad the concussion was. She no doubt had a concussion. I just hoped there was no internal bleeding.

After wrapping a fresh bandage around her head, just in case, I glanced out at the snowfall again. Deadly.

It would be more dangerous for me to try to get her out of here now, I reasoned, than it would be to let her rest and heal and hope the internal damage was not too bad.

The dog had his head on his paws and his eyes closed.

Moving quietly and carefully, not trusting the dog not to wake up and bite off my hand, I checked her pockets. She had no ID. No cell phone. Nothing identifying who she was.

And now that the plane had gone up in flames, there would be no way for me to know unless she told me.

Maybe the dog had ID on him.

I reached over and patted him on the head, waking him up in the process. He watched me with sleepy eyes as I checked his collar.

"Biscuit?" The dog just looked at me and blinked. "Your name is Biscuit?"

Alright. I looked at the silver tag again. An image of an angel was etched on it, beneath his name. I turned the tag over. The name Angel was on the other side.

Angel.

I looked at the girl sleeping in my bed. The name was fitting.

"You're Angel?" I asked softly.

She did not even stir.

I pulled a warm sherpa blanket up to her chin and put a down blanket over her feet.

"Sleep well, Angel," I said.

I stoked up the fire. One thing I had was plenty of firewood.

It looked like Angel, Biscuit, and I would be riding out this storm together.

Then I would have to find a way to get her out of here.

I might be wanting to spend the winter months holed up in a mountain cabin, but Angel certainly would not. Besides, she had to be checked out medically.

Search and rescue should be coming to look for her. In fact, they probably already knew where she had gone down. It was just a matter of time before they found her.

I sat back down in my chair and picked up my book. But I didn't read. I just watched Angel sleep. She was a beautiful princess and I was her guardian for however much time we had before she was rescued.

I would keep her safe. That was something I was good at. Something I could do.

The snow fell silently outside. Encasing us in our own little world.

I contemplated going back out. Looking for others. The pilot maybe. But I didn't want to leave Angel alone.

It was probably selfish of me, but I would let search and rescue find the pilot and anyone else who might have been thrown from the plane before it burst into flames. But there hadn't been anyone else on the plane. I had checked.

But I had Angel to watch over and I took that seriously.

5

CAMILA

I woke with my face buried beneath a wool blanket. It smelled unfamiliar. A little bit like... dog... and wood smoke.

It was quiet. Very quiet. I heard no cars on the road.

Just the crackling of the fire in the fireplace. At least that explained where the scent of wood smoke came from.

But dog?

Opening my eyes, I saw nothing but darkness.

There was something wrapped around my head. I lightly touched what felt like some kind of bandage.

I started to push it away, but then I felt something sticky on my fingertips. Maybe I'd just leave it alone for now.

I lay very still. Listening. Trying to get my bearings on where I was. Nothing felt familiar. Not the firm mattress or the soft blanket.

I rolled over, making everything hurt. Nothing specific, just everything.

Squinting against a faint light, I struggled to see. An iPad. Someone had left an iPad on the nightstand of wherever this was. Someone... I didn't recognize the cover.

Lifting my head, I tried to sit up. There was the glow of a fire, banked low in the fireplace across the room.

It wasn't a big room. It actually looked like a one-room log cabin.

A fireplace on one wall. Windows on either side of the front door. There was a small kitchen area and this bed. One side door that, presumably, went to the bathroom.

The windows were uncovered. Looking out into the pitch dark night.

But… why was I here?

Pressing my hands against my forehead, I tried to remember. I only had a swirl of disjointed images that meant nothing. The memories were fleeting and made no sense as they flitted through my head.

I was sore, pretty much all over and my head ached.

When the door opened, I jumped and pulled the blanket up to my chin.

Someone stepped inside, bringing a swirl of cold air with them, but I couldn't see who it was.

Whoever it was came over to the bed and flipped on a lamp.

I blinked and covered my eyes against the unexpected light.

A man sat in a chair next to the bed.

"Hi," he said, with surprise.

I swallowed. "Hi."

Had I been kidnapped?

"I didn't expect you to be awake," the man said. "My name is Beau."

"You kidnapped me?" I asked, not sure whether to sit still or to try to run.

"What? No." He ran a hand over his face. "You were in an accident."

"What kind of accident?"

"You don't remember?" he asked.

I shook my head.

"Your plane crashed," he said.

"No." I shook my head. Then searched his blue eyes. I did not know this man, but he looked sincere and he did not look dangerous. "What plane?"

Alarm flashed over his face, but he hid it for the most part. "You were in a small jet. It crashed."

"Where?" I asked. Not that that would tell me anything, but I was looking for something to ground myself in time and place.

"Not far from here," he said. "Maybe a mile."

I contemplated that for a moment. "Where is here?"

"Just outside of Whiskey Springs, Colorado."

That should mean something. But it didn't.

"A log cabin," I said. "Yours?"

"For the winter, yes."

"Why would you rent a cabin for the winter?" I asked.

His gaze darted toward the fire, then back to mine. "I wanted some time alone," he said.

I nodded slowly. "So much for that, huh?"

"It's okay," he said.

"What about the others in the plane?"

"Others?"

"I guess." I tried hard to remember, but I didn't even remember being on an airplane, much less crashing.

"How many others were on the plane, Angel?" he asked.

Angel? I looked at him with so many questions. Was that my name then?

A dog came over to jump onto the bed.

"Who is this?" I asked.

"Your dog, Biscuit."

"Right." The dog, oddly enough, was the most familiar thing to me right now.

"Biscuit?" I asked the dog. He barked once, then scooted over to me and licked my face.

I laughed, at least what was almost a laugh.

Beau was watching me.

"How do you feel?" he asked when I looked back at him.

"My head hurts a bit," I said.

"You had quite a bump." He leaned forward and gently touched my forehead where I had felt the stickiness of blood.

"You brought me here," I said.

"Yes. How many others were on the airplane?"

"I don't know." I looked into his eyes.

"What's the last thing you remember?" he asked.

I scrunched up my face. Then shook my head. "I don't know."

"You have to remember something," he said, with a bit of alarm in his tone.

"I really don't."

"Your name?"

"I don't know." I grasped onto the only thing I could. "You called me Angel."

"Does that sound right?"

Did it? I honestly didn't know.

"Do you know your last name?" he persisted.

"I'm not sure I know anything right now," I said.

We looked at each other for a couple of long seconds. Maybe more than that. Maybe a minute. He was a handsome man. Probably about thirty or so. Lean. He had nice eyes. Kind eyes.

"Can I check your bandage?" he asked. "Then maybe you can get some sleep. You'll feel better then."

I nodded. "Thank you for being so kind." Tears welled in my eyes. I wasn't sure why, but they were there.

"You don't have to thank me." His touch was gentle as he removed the bandage, cleaned my wound, and covered it again.

Perhaps not, I thought as I lay my head back against the pillow.

But, it seemed, he knew more about me than I knew about myself.

And that not only had me off balance, it was more than a little disconcerting.

6

BEAU

I sat in a little wooden chair in front of the fire, my feet propped on the hearth.

Somewhere along the way, my plans had gone awry. I had planned to spend the next few months in solitude. To regroup, so to speak, and discover who, exactly I was now.

And then to figure out my next step. I needed a general direction so I would know where to start. But a step in that general direction would be enough for now.

But my complete solitude had been shattered by a plane crashing practically right over my head, missing me perhaps by no more than a mile.

The odds were too astronomical for me to calculate.

I would be hard pressed to be convinced that it was something other than fate that had brought us together. That had put me in charge of this woman's well-being.

A wolf howled in the distance. Biscuit lifted his head, but put it back down and closed his eyes.

I had been outside when she had woken. I was outside because I didn't want to wake her. Using my radio, I had listened for a weather forecast.

The storm, just as I had predicted, had come not only earlier, but also stronger than they expected.

They were advising people to hunker down and shelter in place.

I didn't know what that would do to search and rescue for a plane's distress call. In my experience nothing. In the military, nothing stopped us from doing our job.

But I had to consider the possibility that no one knew where the plane had gone down if they even knew that it had gone down at all.

So there was that.

Then there was Angel herself.

I was worried about her.

She remembered nothing about herself. I don't think she even knew her name until I told her.

The only thing familiar to her seemed to be the dog.

If someone came looking for her, that was one thing, but I wasn't about to take her out in this storm.

She would just have to stay here with me. In my little cabin.

I had to admit that I really did not mind so much.

Angel was pleasant to look at. Beautiful, in fact.

And after she got some rest, she would feel better and most likely her memory would come back.

I'd planned on going to town for provisions, but now I couldn't go. Couldn't leave her. The storm was too bad anyway, so it was just as well that I wasn't tempted. Having Angel here would keep me from being restless and careless and putting my own life on the line trying to get to town.

I had enough food to last for both of us.

I was quite relaxed, thinking about how I didn't mind her being here, when she screamed.

I jumped up, turning my chair over backwards.

Biscuit got to his feet, standing in the bed. My bed.

I hurried to her bedside, but she was still asleep.

Then she cried out and tears ran down her cheeks, but still, she did not wake up.

I shot Biscuit a challenging look, then sat on the bed next to her and gathered her in my arms.

Cradling her close, I soothed her as she cried and whimpered in her sleep. Biscuit watched me, but did not interfere.

Finally, she settled back into a peaceful sleep. I gently laid her back and brought the blanket back up to her chin.

Biscuit laid down next to her.

It was the first time I'd ever been envious of a dog, for God's sake.

I went back to my chair in front of the fire and settled my own nerves down. Angel was such a little thing. And getting past the scent of jet fuel and wet dog, she smelled like jasmine and vanilla.

I was still worried about her not remembering anything. Most people remembered *something* after an accident.

But I'd much rather her scream and cry in her sleep than to slip into a coma. I'd seen that happen, too.

If she didn't remember basics like her name in the morning, then I would allow myself to be worried. Not that there was anything I could do about it. Nothing anyone could do about it, really. Nothing except to be supportive and make sure she didn't get into any trouble. To make sure she got plenty of rest.

I could do those things. There was nowhere for her to go and nothing for her to get into trouble with out here in the middle of the woods in a snowstorm.

Except maybe for me.

I had to keep my hands off of her.

I wasn't dating anyone and hadn't been for a couple of years. So spending time in close quarters with her was going to be a bit torturous for me.

But I was a trained soldier. I could keep my hands to myself.

I could behave.

I just had to make sure I didn't slip.

Finding some extra blankets and a pillow in the bathroom closet, I made myself a pallet on the floor next to her bed.

If she woke in the night, I would know it. And I would be right here to take care of anything she might need.

7

CAMILA

I dreamed fiercely that night. I dreamed I was alone in an airplane, piloting it myself. And something went wrong. Very wrong. And I was going down. Crashing. Nothing I did could stop it from happening.

I screamed, but someone was there to comfort me. Someone with kind, strong arms. Everything in my head was fuzzy and I didn't want to wake up. I wanted to stay asleep, but I wanted to dream something pleasant. Somehow my mind cooperated.

I dreamed about playing badminton with my grandfather in his backyard. There were butterflies around us. One landed on my shoulder. Grandpa took my hand and told me it was good luck for a butterfly to land on someone.

Then I had another dream. This one about running along the beach, holding Daddy's hand. We were flying a kite. It went so high in the sky I could barely see it over my shoulder. We were both laughing.

"It's flying, Daddy," I laughed. "I wish I could fly like that."

"You can," he said. "One day. You can fly as high as you want."

Then I woke up. My heart racing as though I had actually been running. I was still in the one room cabin. But instead of darkness behind the windows, the cloudy light of early morning spilled through.

The dog was licking my face. Was that what had woken me?

The man... Beau... said the dog's name was Biscuit. An interesting name for a dog.

Then I recognized the scent of breakfast.

"Good morning," Beau said, bringing a tray of food to me.

The tray held a plate of eggs, bacon, and toast.

"How do you like your coffee?" he asked.

I shrugged and held out my hand.

He handed me a steaming mug of black coffee. I took one sip and scrunched my face.

"I don't think I like it like this," I said, setting the mug down on the tray.

"I didn't think so," he said. "Be right back."

While he was gone, I finished off the water bottle. Then I picked up a piece of bacon and took a bite.

"Here's the closest thing to a latte I could get." He handed me the mug of light brown creamy looking coffee.

"Thank you." I took a sip. "Good."

He picked up the empty water bottle. "A little thirsty?" he asked.

"I guess so," I said a bit sheepishly.

He sat down in the chair next to the bed and watched as I took a bite of the egg. Closed my eyes.

"This is really good," I said. Either that or I was absolutely starving.

"I fed Biscuit," he said. "No dog food, but I cooked him some hamburger meat."

I smiled at him. "You're very kind."

He shrugged. Then leaned forward, resting his elbows on his knees.

"Do you know what day it is?" he asked.

I actually had no idea whatsoever. I shook my head.

He sighed. "Your last name?"

I shook my head again, sipped the hot coffee, then took another bite of bacon. I didn't tell him, but it seemed like I had not had bacon in a very long time.

Just another one of those things I couldn't explain.

"You don't seem worried," he said. "about your loss of memory."

I took the mug in both hands and sat back. "I have too much to worry about," I said. "If I start worrying, I might be overwhelmed."

"I get that," he said. "I think your bandage can come off."

"Okay," I said, setting the tray aside. "Where are you from Beau?"

He smiled a little as he removed the bandage and checked my wound. "How's the headache?"

"It's a little better. I can keep my eyes open now."

"Good," he said. "I was born in Dallas, but I didn't grow up anywhere in particular."

"You have no place to call home?" Something about that tore at my heart. Although I couldn't remember anything about my own family, I felt bad for him not having anyone.

"Military," he said, as though that explained everything.

"What about now? Where is your family?"

"Last I heard, my mother is in Italy."

"Oh." Last I heard couldn't be a good thing.

Then he latched onto my gaze. "Where is your family?" he said.

I felt tears welling in my eyes, but I quickly blinked them away. "I don't know," I said. "I have fleeting images, but nothing I can see clearly enough to recognize."

"What else are you experiencing?"

"It seems like the more I try to remember, the further the memories slip out of my reach."

He didn't say anything for a moment. Then he stood up and held out a hand.

"Come here," he said. "I want to show you something."

I put my hand in his and allowed him to help me get to my feet.

He led me to the door, Biscuit at our heels.

We stepped outside and I had to catch my breath.

Snowflakes were coming down like light misty rain.

But all around, as far as the eye could see, was a winter wonderland.

8

BEAU

I liked the snow. And when I was in the mood for it, I liked the snowstorms.

I'd seen a lot of places—pretty places—but I had never seen a place as beautiful as where I was right now.

It wasn't the untouched blanket of snow covering the ground. It wasn't the soft flakes coming down. It wasn't the view of the bubbling river below. Water flowing through the banks of snow.

It was all of that. All of that with Angel. Because of Angel.

Without Angel, it would just be ordinary snow. Pretty, but ordinary.

With her it was just magical.

She walked out into the falling snow, turned up her face, and smiled as the snowflakes covered her lashes, her hair.

Even Biscuit, whom I had already taken for a walk in the snow earlier, seemed to be infected by her wonder.

He sprinted around her, barking at the snowflakes. He was really just a puppy, I realized, in spite of how disciplined he seemed to be at protecting Angel.

If I didn't know better, I would almost think neither of them had ever seen snow before.

I hadn't paid much attention to it, but her accent was southern. Like mine. Not too southern. Texas.

Angel was from Texas. I'd stake my military training on it.

Speaking of military training or medical training to be more specific. I knew that I needed to let her memory come back naturally.

There were some who would say it was good to provide prompts and reminders, but from what I had seen in the field, pushing too hard only led to frustration which caused the person to have even more trouble getting their memory back.

"It's beautiful," she said, turning back to face me.

"I think so, too," I said. "But it's causing us a bit of a problem. We're right in the middle of a blizzard. So I can't get you out of here right now."

"I don't mind," she said, then stopped. "But you wanted time alone."

"I did, it's true. But I don't mind you being here."

She smiled again and bit her lip.

"But," I said, holding out a hand again. "We're not dressed for it."

She put her hand in mine and we went back inside the cabin. I wrapped a blanket around her shoulders and together we sat on two wooden chairs in front of the fire. I put a blanket on the floor in front of the fireplace for Biscuit.

"You have a lot of firewood," she pointed out.

"Good thing," I said. Firewood was stacked in neat rows halfway to the ceiling to the right of the fireplace. I found it rather decorative.

"Did you chop all this yourself?"

"Unfortunately, yes."

"Hmm."

We sat in silence for a few minutes.

"So what do you do out here besides chop firewood and cook?"

"My plan was to use the time to think."

She looked at me with what had to be curiosity.

"That's a lot of thinking," she said.

I laughed. "You're right."

"So how's it going? All the thinking?"

"Taking my time," I said. "Sometimes it's best not to rush it."

She nodded. "I think that sounds like a good plan." She adjusted the blanket around her and sat back, closing her eyes.

"Whoever owns this cabin should really spring for a sofa," she said.

"I'll let the landlord know."

The fire crackled sending little sparks up the chimney. It was snowing again. Big snowflakes now, making it hard to see outside.

But I didn't mind. I was content to just sit here next to Angel.

As far as I was concerned, everything was perfect.

9

___

CAMILA

*B*eau turned on the radio so the news and weather could play in the background. Mostly music, though, now, eighties music.

I recognized the music, oddly enough. How was it I knew music and not my own name?

When I woke from a nap, Beau was chopping vegetables.

I sat at the table and watched him.

"You're good at that," I said.

"I get tired of restaurant food," he said, tossing everything into a big pot on the stove.

"Makes sense."

"I hope you don't mind vegetarian pasta," he said. "Saving the chicken and beef for Biscuit."

"I don't mind," I said. "I think I prefer it."

"That's interesting," he said, adding a touch of wine to the sauce.

"It's just an... impression," I said. "I can't remember anything in particular."

"It'll come back," he said.

I believed him. Maybe because I wanted to believe him.

He seemed so competent and confident. If he said my memory was going to get better, then it would.

I jumped and we both froze when someone knocked on the door.

Beau opened a kitchen drawer. Took something out and closed the drawer back. "Who is it?" he called out.

"Neighbor," A man said. "Just checking in."

Beau went to the door, opened it, and stepped out.

I caught only snatches of their conversation.

"Bad storm. We don't have service."

"Guess I've been lucky so far."

"Need anything?"

"I'm good."

A few minutes later, the man left and Beau came back inside.

"Everything okay?" I asked.

"Just a neighbor checking in. Said power's out everywhere."

"We have power."

"So far." He went to the stove and stirred the pasta. "He didn't say anything about the plane crash."

"And you didn't tell him."

He turned and looked at me. "No."

"Why not?" I asked.

He seemed to consider. "I don't know. I guess because I don't know him."

She nodded. "Good."

"I know you must be ready to get out of here."

I shook my head. I didn't feel ready to get out of here. I was somehow content. "I'm okay," I said.

"Want to play a game of cards while that simmers?" he asked.

"Sure."

It didn't take long to discover that I was quite good at blackjack.

"I think you're a little card shark," he said, indicating the nice little stack of matches I had accumulated.

"Maybe I'm a dealer," I said.

He looked at me sideways. "I don't think so."

"Why not?" I asked.

"You don't have the look," he said, shuffling the cards.

I laughed. "And what look is that?"

He dealt again. "I don't think you hang out at casinos."

"And you do?" I asked.

"No." We both had two face cards. "But I've known guys who do."

"Split," I said, moving my cards apart.

He did the same.

I won both hands while he won one.

"That's it," he said. "I can't play with you anymore. You're a professional card player."

"No, I'm not," I said with a laugh. "You said I didn't hang out at casinos."

"I might be wrong about that," he said. "but you don't work at one."

I did know cards, I mused as he finished making the pasta. He hadn't had to teach me how to play. I knew about splitting cards and doubling down.

From the last hour, I would say that I'm not someone who is afraid to take risks.

I couldn't help but wonder what other hidden talents and traits I might have that I didn't know about.

And I was curious what kind of person I would turn out to be.

10

BEAU

*A*ngel was a good eater, as my grandmother would say. She finished off her whole plate of pasta and didn't even pretend that she was one of those girls who starved themselves to be thin. She must be one of the naturally thin ones.

We drank water, not wine, since she had a concussion.

I was just washing the last of the dishes when the electricity blinked once, then blinked out for good.

It was cloudy with the snow, so we were immediately immersed in shadows and it seemed to get colder immediately.

"Do you have a flashlight?" Angel asked.

"I have a flashlight and..." I reached into one of the kitchen cabinets and brought out a battery-operated lantern.

"Nice," she said, going to stand in front of the fireplace. "It's going to get cold, isn't it?" she asked.

"We have enough firewood to last awhile."

Though in all truthfulness, it could take weeks to get electricity back on out here. The utility company took care of the town first, then worked their way out.

I could chop more if I needed to, of course.

She pulled her matches out of her pocket and laid them out in little stacks.

"What are you doing?" I asked, trying not to laugh.

"Counting my money," she said with a straight face.

"I see." I seriously hoped she was joking and that this wasn't some belief she had developed from the concussion.

But then she grinned up at me. "Wondering what I could cash them in for. Maybe a blanket."

"Ha." I held up the box of matches, hiding my relief. "Unfortunately you're not in the best market right now."

"Oh well," she shrugged. "Maybe we can play again tomorrow."

"What, you don't want to try to take the rest of the house matches?"

"Looks like the house might be needing them," she said. "So I'll give the house a break for tonight."

"Alright," I said, sitting next to her.

I put a hand on her forehead under the guise of checking her temperature. In truth it was just excuse to touch her. Already, I was feeling comfortable about taking her hand. Touching her face. I reminded myself to keep my hands to myself.

Angel wrapped herself in her blanket.

She was right. It was going to get cold. I could already tell that this old cabin didn't have a lot of insulation.

"When you aren't here," she asked. "Thinking. What do you like to do?"

"That's actually what I'm here to... think about. To figure out."

"Surely there's something."

"I put all my energy into my work."

"You like to read," she said.

"True. But I'm not sure that really counts as an activity."

"In my book, it does," she said. "Pun not intended."

"Any idea what you like to do besides play cards?" I asked. "Needlepoint maybe."

"Needlepoint?" She echoed, with a bit of offense in her tone. "That's rather sexist, don't you think?"

I shrugged. "Men do it. It's a thing."

"Ok," she said. "When you start doing needlepoint, I'll do it, too."

There was a challenging gleam in her eyes that I found interesting and maybe a little bit telling. This girl did not back down from a challenge.

"I wonder why I was on an airplane," she said, looking over at Biscuit sleeping in front of the fire.

"Could be anything," I said.

"But airplanes don't normally fly in blizzards. It must have been some kind of emergency." Her brow creased.

"The storm got here sooner than they expected." I wanted to smooth the worry from her brow.

"I suppose," she said, staring into the fire.

Whether it was a good thing or not, she was starting to think. Maybe even to figure some things out about herself.

I should be happy for her. But I selfishly wasn't ready for things to change. I rather liked getting to know her. Discovering things about her as she did.

She could be someone completely different than the girl she was right now. But it didn't matter. So far there wasn't anything I didn't like about her.

And no matter what happened, my peaceful solitary interlude was shattered.

11

CAMILA

$\mathcal{I}$ woke shivering.

Even though I was under blankets, I didn't think I had ever been this cold.

The only light in the cabin came from the flickering fire in the fireplace. I just wasn't close enough to benefit from whatever heat the flames gave off.

Climbing out from beneath the pile of blankets, I wrapped the top one around me and put my feet on the cold floor.

I grabbed a second blanket and headed single-mindedly toward the fireplace. Like a moth to a flame.

And I promptly tripped over something. Biscuit. Biscuit was huddled on his own blanket in front of the fire.

But I didn't hit the floor. Instead, I landed right on top of Beau.

"Whoa," he said, guiding me to the floor next to him. "What are you doing?"

"C-c-cold." My teeth chattered over the word.

"You've got all the blankets," he said.

I just sat and shivered.

"Hold on," he said. "Let me fix this."

I inched closer to the flames as he did whatever he went off to do.

"Okay," he said, taking my arm. "Come sit next to me over here."

He'd brought all the blankets and made a pallet out of them. I sat on a soft furry blanket while he wrapped blankets around my shoulders.

"Better?" he asked.

I shook my head.

He set an iron kettle filled with water in the fireplace. A few minutes later, he poured some of the steaming water into a mug and handed it to me.

I wrapped my fingers around the warm mug and breathed in the steam.

It helped. Some.

He sat next to me, wrapped the blankets around both of us.

"Body heat is the best," he said, pulling me close and wrapping his arms around me.

I nodded. Right now I didn't care what it took. I just wanted to stop shivering.

A few minutes later, I took a deep breath and let it out slowly. I'd stopped shivering.

"Better?" he asked.

"Much," I said. "Thank you."

I laughed when Biscuit came over and nuzzled his way beneath the blankets with us.

"He wants to be part of the family," Beau said.

My breath hitched a little at his words.

Part of the family.

Oddly enough, that was exactly what it felt like right now. It felt like we were a little family.

I knew it wasn't real. I knew it wouldn't last.

But I also knew that I wanted it to.

I leaned my head against Beau's chest and he rested his chin on the top of my head.

I could feel his heart beating or maybe it was mine. I think it was both of ours.

Our hearts seemed to be beating as one.

He kissed the top of my head and I shifted ever so slightly so that my forehead was next to his chin. He shifted, too, and kissed me on that tender spot next to my eye.

My lips parted and my breath was coming in shallow gasps. Not wanting him to move away, I sat very still. Not moving a muscle.

I'm not sure how long we sat like this, keeping each other warm.

But then he hugged me even closer.

And when he did, his lips ended up at the corner of my mouth.

Shivers ran through me. I closed my eyes and waited.

I didn't know who I was. For all I knew I had a boyfriend or was engaged or was married.

It felt like I was about to tip over the edge of... something.

Whoever I was right now was falling for Beau.

The problem was I didn't who I really was.

Once I figured out who I was, what would happen to what I felt for Beau? Would it just vanish to be replaced by my memories? Or would these new feelings continue, perhaps even overriding what I felt for someone else?

It was too complicated to think about. It just made my head hurt.

And it didn't do much for my heart either.

Right now my heart ached for Beau. I couldn't get close enough to him. Even if it was wrong, it was what I felt.

Was it technically cheating if I didn't know who I was supposed to love?

Ah hell.

I opened my eyes and stared at the flickering flames.

There was a possibility that my memory might never come back. That I would always be who I was right now.

If that was the case, it made no sense to turn away from what I was feeling for Beau. None whatsoever.

I had to live in the moment.

I had been the sole survivor of a plane crash and then I'd nearly frozen to death.

It was a wakeup call, if nothing else was.

Tomorrow may never come.

I shifted again at the same time he did and our lips touched. Neither of us moved.

12

BEAU

I'd told myself to keep my hands to myself.

But then she'd simply fallen into my arms. I could hardly let her freeze to death just because I needed to be cautious.

She had been trembling like a leaf. I kicked myself for thinking she would be warm way over there in the bed, even under all those blankets.

I'd been sitting here warm in front of the blazing fire. On the floor, but still warm.

She was warm now. We both were.

That didn't give me license to kiss her.

The flames licked at the wood, and a log fell, sending sparks up the chimney. They could land someplace on the snow, but would probably go cold as soon as they reached the cold air at the top of the chimney.

We were ensconced in our own little world. Right now, in fact, she was my whole world.

Her lips were soft and smooth as rose petals. I savored the feel of her against me. The feel of her lips against mine.

We weren't going anywhere. We could be stuck here for days.

My solitude time had morphed into something completely different. Now it was a romantic interlude.

I was hooked.

I could sit right here like this with my lips against hers for the rest of my life and be content.

Or for a few minutes anyway.

Then she went and did it. She put her arms around me and shifted the kiss deeper.

I couldn't take all the blame. After all, it took two. Right?

Our lips melded together in what could only be called a perfect kiss.

Biscuit whimpered and I pulled back a little.

"You're beautiful," I said.

"I don't even know who I am," she said. I heard the confusion and sadness in her voice.

"It doesn't matter," I said, lightly touching her cheek. "I know who you are right this minute."

"I'm not sure I do," she said, shifting her gaze to the fire.

She was wrestling with the memory loss. I couldn't even imagine having my memories wiped out, although, actually it might not be such a bad thing for me.

A tree crashed to the ground outside. Both of us, Biscuit, too, looked toward the window.

"We're safe here?" she asked.

"There's a pistol in the top kitchen drawer," I said.

"Right. Military."

"Do you know how to use it?" Did she even know whether she knew?

"Of course. Just point and pull the trigger." She sounded a bit annoyed that I would even ask.

I hugged her close. "I like you," I said. "No matter who you turn out to be."

"Will I forget you when my memory comes back?" she asked.

"If you're in a dissociative fugue maybe," I said. "but most people don't forget when their memory comes back."

"That's good," she said, but she didn't sound certain.

"Angel," I said. "It's okay. Whatever happens, I'm here."

She looked at me closely, searching my eyes.

"Beau," she said.

I gently cupped her cheek with my hand and kissed her on the forehead. I was having a hard time not touching her.

She put a hand on my arm and looked at me, her face full of uncertainty.

"What's wrong?"

"I don't think my name is Angel."

13

CAMILA

*B*eau handed me a mug of hot, steaming water. Although it was too hot to drink, the steam warmed my skin and the mug warmed my hands.

The fire in the fireplace gave off enough heat to keep us warm, but sitting snuggled up next to Beau made it all that much warmer. Pleasantly so.

I might be feeling a little bit too comfortable snuggled up next to him, a perfect stranger, like this.

I picked up one of the crackers he'd put on a plate with some cheese.

He sat back down, settling the blanket back around us.

"Okay," he said, picking up a piece of cheese. "I'm ready now. If your name isn't Angel, then what is it?"

I shrugged. "I don't know."

He picked up a cracker. Looked at me crossways. "But it isn't Angel."

"I don't think so," I said. "It doesn't feel right."

"I get that," he said. "You just now realized this?"

"Maybe," I said. "I can't explain it." I scratched Biscuit's head. Looked at his collar and understood how he had come up with the name for me. "I think maybe Angel is a company?"

It came out as a question because I had no thoughts to back up the feeling.

He nodded. "It's possible. I'd look it up but there's no cell phone service out here."

"It's okay," I said, leaning my head against his shoulder. "Maybe it's better if we don't know right now."

"I agree," he said, kissing me on the cheek. "It feels sort of like time stopped."

I looked up at him. "It does, kinda."

"Do you mind?" He leaned back on one elbow, letting in the cold air.

"Yes," I said. "It's cold." I grabbed at the blankets and wrapped them around me again.

"Not that," he said with a little laugh. "Do you mind that time feels like it stopped?"

I looked over at him. At his handsome features. In this particular moment, he looked a little bit vulnerable.

"No," I said. "I don't mind. I actually kinda like it."

He sat up, disturbing my blankets again. "I have a theory."

"What kind of theory?" I asked, sampling some more of the cheese.

"I think you're from Texas."

I froze. A cracker halfway to my lips.

"Texas." It rolled off my tongue with a familiarity I hadn't expected.

"What?" he asked. "Are you remembering something?"

I shook my head. Set the cracker back down. I didn't want it after all.

I wasn't remembering anything. It was just another one of those vague feelings.

"Why do you say Texas?" I asked.

"I recognize the accent," he said with a shrug. "military."

"Right." It was odd that Texas seemed so familiar... so... right.

Maybe I was from Texas.

There was only one problem with figuring out who I was.

I wasn't sure I was ready to know.

Knowing who I was meant the possible loss of my relationship with Beau.

If I was already in a relationship, then I would have to let go of him.

Maybe if I didn't think about it.

"Do you mind if we turn on the radio?" I asked. "See what the weather is doing."

"Not at all," he said, reaching over and turning on the local station.

Maybe if I just didn't think, everything would be okay.

I let my mind go blank as Beau moved past the static to find the local station.

14

BEAU

*B*eing a paramedic in search and rescue, I'd gone through a unique kind of training. Different from not only most soldiers, but also most paramedics. One of the things that had made my training unique was that my best friend in the unit had been a psychiatrist by the name of Don.

I'd say that I learned a lot from him.

Unfortunately, he had not made it out. I missed him. And sometimes I still had dreams about him. I even dreamed sometimes that we had conversations on the phone. I knew the conversations weren't real, even when they were happening, but they *felt* real. I guess he was still a presence in my life. Maybe always would be.

If he were here, I could ask him about Angel. He would know what to do. He was one of the smartest men I'd ever known.

I tossed another log on the fire, sending a spray of sparks everywhere.

Music blasted on the radio. No news yet. Tired of the noise, I reached over and turned it down.

I tucked a strand of hair out of Angel's eyes. She smiled up at me with slightly swollen lips.

"I know you don't remember, but since you don't think your name is Angel, what do you think it is?" I asked, returning to our earlier conversation.

"I don't know," she said, scrunching up her nose.

"Don't think. Just quick. What's your name?"

"Camila," she said. Her eyes widened, putting a hand over her mouth. "Why would I say that?"

"Maybe it's your name."

"But I don't know." She shook her head.

"It's okay," I said. "Don't stress. But…" I hugged her close.

"But what?"

"What should I call you?"

She bit her lip, her eyes moist.

"Angel is okay," she said. "I've gotten kinda used to it."

"It rather suits you," I said. "Simply because you're as beautiful as an angel."

When she just rolled her eyes in response, my heart tripped a little bit harder. I had a feeling this humbleness was another facet of her personality. And, like everything else about her, I found it charming.

"I'll be right back," she said, heading to the restroom.

I sat back and watched the flames. I could most definitely get used to this. This being with her.

The little jingle that signaled a news bulletin was coming caught my attention.

"Good evening everyone. We just got word that a single passenger jet lost contact in this area yesterday. The manifest shows that the only soul on board was the pilot by the name of Camila Worthington. If anyone has seen or heard anything that could lead to her recovery, please call the station as soon as possible. There's a hefty reward for anyone who finds her. Help us out folks. There's a blizzard out there. Help Camila's family by bringing their girl home."

I just stared at the radio.

Camila Worthington.

She knew her name but she didn't know she knew it.

A pilot.

Angel… Camila… was a pilot.

I reached over and switched the radio off.

Even though I knew, I had no way of getting her out of here. No way to contact anyone.

I'd liked it that way when I came out here to be alone.

But now…

I sat back. Considered.

She was here. She was safe.

When the weather permitted, I would get her out of here.

The bathroom door opened and she dashed out, rushing back to her seat on the pallet. She snuggled back beneath the blankets and pressed her cheek against my chest.

"It's cold in there," she said and I felt her shivering.

"I'll keep you warm, sweetie," I said, pulling her close. *Camila.* I would have to get used to calling her that.

Now all I had to do was to figure out how and when to tell her.

And once again, I wished I had my buddy, Don, back.

He would know.

But this time I had to figure it out for myself.

15

CAMILA

I woke the next morning snuggled beneath a pile of blankets, a large fire roaring in the fireplace, wrapped in Beau's arms. Biscuit was asleep at our feet.

I wondered when Beau had gotten up to put wood on the fire and how he had done it without waking me.

Not wanting to move, I lay still and listened to the birds singing their morning song outside the window.

The snow must have stopped. Everything was so quiet. Like there was a blanket over the earth.

I decided right then that I liked winter in the mountains.

That revelation came with a healthy dose of respect for both the season and the mountains.

I was fortunate to be alive right now. And if Beau hadn't found me, I would be out there, probably frozen to death.

Texas. Had I been on an airplane from Texas? It was possible. There could be a million reasons why.

Whatever it was, I hoped it wasn't anything too terribly important.

And again, I wondered why the pilot would have flown with a storm coming in.

Beau had said the storm came earlier than predicted. Flying was mostly science, but there was an art aspect to it also.

I shook my head. But what did I know? I was merely speculating. I was probably a librarian from Houston.

Ah. That would explain how I thought I knew so much about things. A librarian would know a lot about a lot of different things. Random things. Like weather and flying. Blackjack. That the angel on Biscuit's collar had something to do with some kind of agency.

I'd told Beau my name was Camila. Now that Beau had been calling me Angel, Camila sounded a little bit strange, but, I guess, it was possible. Anything was possible.

"A penny for your thoughts," Beau said.

"Good morning," I said, blinking and looking over at him. "How long have you been awake?"

"Not long." He glanced toward the window. "I think the snow stopped."

"I agree," I said.

He kissed me lightly on the lips.

"You looked like you were deep in thought," he said.

I nodded. "I think I know who I am.

"Oh?" Beau sat up. "Who are you?"

"Camila. A librarian from Houston."

"What makes you think that?" he asked.

"Well, Camila because… it just popped in my head and I don't think it's Angel." I pulled the blanket closer. "I think I'm a librarian because I know random things like blackjack." I stopped at that, not wanting to tell him everything I was thinking.

"Why Houston?" he asked.

I shrugged. "Feels right. You know?"

"Alright, then, Camila from Houston," he said. "How about I make us some breakfast, then we take a walk. See what the damage is."

"Sounds good. How are you going to cook?"

"You'll see," he said with a little wink.

I sat back, watching him pull out a kettle and some eggs. "It's so quiet."

He nodded. "I always know when it snowed overnight. It's like a blanket settled over the world and everything is silent."

"You really like it out here," I said. "The quiet."

"I do."

"But you don't live here."

He shook his head. Deftly cracked an egg.

"Where do you live?"

"That's one of the things I'm planning on figuring out this winter."

I wrapped my arms around my knees. "You're kinda like me," I said. "But for different reasons."

"How so?"

"Well…" I mused. "I don't know where I'm headed and neither do you."

He stopped what he was doing and stared at me. "That's an interesting observation. Except I know where I've been."

I shrugged.

"Sometimes I wouldn't mind forgetting some of my past," he said, a shadow passing over his features.

"I can't even imagine what it must have been like overseas."

"There were some moments," he said, stirring the eggs, then quickly changed the subject. "You're sure you're a librarian?"

"I'm not sure of much of anything," I said. Thinking about the painful things he must have seen as a paramedic put a damper on my spirits.

I decided that both of us would be better off focusing on the here and now than either our past or our future.

16

BEAU

"Be still," I said.

Trying to bundle Angel... Camila... up in one of my coats was next to impossible.

First of all, she looked lost in it. I could fit two, maybe three of her in there and I wasn't that big.

"I am being still," she said.

I stopped with one of her sleeves halfway rolled up and looked up her. Then I just laughed. Biscuit was nuzzling the coat, making it shake.

And then the two of us were laughing like loons.

Quite a pair we were. Me who didn't know where I was headed and her who didn't know where she had been.

But right now we were a good match for each other.

When I decided she was sufficiently bundled, I opened the door and Biscuit dashed out ahead of us, sending up a spray of snow beneath his feet.

I subtly guided her in the opposite direction of the plane crash. That was not something she needed to see right now.

Instead, we took the path that led into town. It was about an hour's walk, so I didn't plan on us going all the way into town.

As far as I was concerned, we were just out for a stroll.

I took her hand and laced my fingers loosely with her.

The sunlight glinted off the untouched snow weighing heavy on the tree limbs. Only a couple of trees were on the ground and some of them were drooping, but most of the trees in this part of the country were hardy enough to withstand anything the weather could throw at them.

Camila's attention was drawn to a jet passing overhead.

I should tell her.

But, one, I didn't know for sure. It *could* be a coincidence that she thought her name was Camila and there was a missing pilot with the same name.

That was impossible, of course, and I knew it.

But I didn't want to do anything to damage her psyche.

So I kept my mouth shut and braced myself for the moment when she figured it out. When she did, she would most likely want go home as soon as possible.

So I would cherish every moment we had.

Reminded myself to live in the now. Not in my past and not in some future no one could predict.

There was a faint possibility that she would never remember who she was.

If that happened, I would have to tell her. To tell someone. It would be the ethical thing to do. I couldn't keep that kind of information to myself.

Just how long, I mused, should I wait?

It actually looked like the path was clear enough to get to town. Maybe today I should take her to town and give the authorities the chance to find out if she was indeed Camila Worthington.

Biscuit circled around to chase a chipmunk before coming back to walk between us, nuzzling our hands.

Just one day.

She smiled when she caught me looking at her. I squeezed her hand and smiled back.

Yes. Just one day.

I wanted just one day to spend with her.

If she figured it out before that, then so be it.

I would cross that bridge when and if I came to it.

Tomorrow. Tomorrow we would go into town and deal with letting everyone know who she was. Get her to a doctor. Report the crash.

My heart broke just a little bit knowing that with the storm over, my time with her was limited.

Here and now, Beau. Here and now.

17

CAMILA

"*I*s this the path to town?" I asked.

"Yes."

I glanced over at Beau. He seemed preoccupied and suddenly not very talkative.

"It looks like it's clear," I said.

He nodded. "Agreed."

"How far is it?" I asked.

"Less than an hour."

I nodded. So, if we were that close and the path was clear enough, we could walk straight into town.

And then what?

Beau said I'd been in a plane crash. I remembered nothing about it. Had to take his word for it.

Then everyone would know that I was Camila, librarian from Houston.

They put me on another plane and send me home. But I didn't know where home was.

Right now home was here. In the cabin with Beau and Biscuit.

I didn't want to go to Houston or anywhere else.

I wanted to stay right here. With him.

As far as I was concerned, I could always be Angel.

A helicopter flew over, not far from us.

I instinctively ducked my head down.

Maybe the helicopter was out to look for the plane that crashed. The plane I had been on. They would find it. Then they would find me.

And someone would figure out that my name was not really Angel. I didn't know how they would figure it out, I just knew they would.

Maybe I wouldn't tell them.

Beau saw the helicopter, too, but he didn't say anything.

"Can we go back now?" I asked. "I'm feeling kinda tired."'

"Of course," Beau said, stopping and turning around without hesitating. Still holding my hand, I pivoted with him.

And we were walking in the other direction—back toward the cabin.

I smiled.

"What is it?" he asked.

"Nothing," I said.

He squeezed my hand.

"You're not ready to go into town either," I said, brushing spray of snow that fell from the trees above us off my sleeve.

"No," he said. "I'm guess I'm not."

"I would think you would be," I said. "so you can get back to your thinking."

He laughed. "I don't think I'll be getting much thinking done right now."

"You could," I said.

"Maybe."

We walked in silence until I saw a little tendril of smoke up ahead.

Biscuit barked once and took off toward the cabin.

"Biscuit is ready to get home, too," I said, then bit my lip. I hadn't meant to call the cabin home out loud.

"Probably hungry," Beau said.

"Probably."

I smiled to myself as we walked the rest of the way back to the cabin.

My heart felt light.

I didn't even know who I was and I felt like I was flying on top of the world.

I didn't want to be anywhere else.

I didn't want to be anyone else.

18

BEAU

I found an old scrabble game stashed in the closet. One of the previous renters must have left it behind. Camila proved to be a formidable opponent at that, too.

She had a lot of talents. From blackjack to scrabble to being an airplane pilot.

As she studied her letters, trying to make a word, I tried to picture her in a cockpit. I was having a hard time with it.

She had a very feminine demeanor and overall moves and when she smiled, it made my heart flutter like a schoolboy.

To put it simply, I was enchanted by her.

"Fifty-eight points," she said, looking up with delight on her face.

"I should just concede," I said as I wrote her points down. "You've got twice as many points as I do."

"Just lucky," she said with a little shrug.

I shook my head as I studied my own letters. "More than luck," I said, playing the first word I came up with.

We played by candlelight and the light of the fireplace. I contemplated opening a bottle of wine.

"I think you're just letting me win," she said.

"Why would I do that?"

"I don't know," she said, "but look." She pointed at the board. "You could have played right here."

"You're right," I said. "I didn't see that."

But I knew and she knew that I hadn't exactly looked hard enough.

"I don't think you're putting forth your best effort," she said.

"You're right," I admitted. "I'm a little distracted."

"Distracted by... the flickering flames?"

"Nah ah."

"Distracted by... the fact that Biscuit wants to go outside for his business?"

I laughed. "No. But maybe I should be."

"Distracted by... the beauty of the moonlight shimmering off the new fallen snow?"

I glanced toward the window. "Maybe. If I could see it."

She looked at me sideways and when she blinked her long thick lashes at me, I felt shaken to the core.

The girl wasn't even wearing a stitch of makeup, but she was more beautiful than any woman I had ever laid eyes on.

"Maybe," I said. "I'm distracted by..." I shoved the scrabble board aside and slid her to me. "you."

She laughed as I kissed her on the cheek.

"I don't mean to be distracting," she said, but her expression said otherwise.

"No?"

She shook her head.

"It's a good thing," I said. My lips were so close to hers our breath mingled. So close that if either one of us moved even just a little, our lips would touch.

Her breath hitched.

"Now you're distracting me," she said on a breath.

"Good," I said. "Because that is my intent."

Then I closed the distance between us and placed my lips against hers.

She sighed.

Torture. She was torturing me.

"Were you sent here to torture me?" I asked.

"Torture? I don't know what you mean."

"Then I guess I'm the only one falling head over heels," I said.

"I don't think so," she said. Then she smiled. "But I do think you might be a little slow to catch up."

It took me a second to understand her meaning.

"I'm all caught up, Angel," I said. "And I'm way out ahead of you."

"We all win," she said. "and we all get prizes."

I'd heard that phrase before.

It had been one of Don's favorite phrases. He said that sometimes a person just needed someone to listen to them. *It's not about what psychological technique we use, it's just having someone to listen.*

The phrase did not really apply here, but it just took me by surprise that my buddy and the girl I was crushing on would utter the same phrase.

"What's wrong?" she asked.

I realized that I hadn't responded. That I had just zoned out, staring into space.

I sat back on my haunches and, scrubbing a hand across my face, apologized. "Sorry. I was just thinking about my buddy."

She sat up, too.

"Your friend in the war?"

"Yeah," I said with a quick glance at her. "How did you know?"

"Lucky guess," she said. "I don't really know."

Oh hell. Surely she wasn't a psychologist, too.

"Want to tell me what happened?" she asked.

"No," I said quickly. Too quickly.

She wrapped the blanket closer around her and looked away.

19

CAMILA

The sun was down now, leaving just the glow from the fireplace to light the cabin. That and the two little candles Beau had lit. I don't think the candles had been designed for giving off light.

Biscuit shifted in his sleep. He'd need to go out soon for his walk.

Seeing the dazed look on Beau's face, had shaken me. It reminded me of how I had felt when I first woke up in Beau's cabin. Of how I felt when he told me I had been in a plane crash.

Reaching out, I put a hand on his cheek.

"I think Biscuit needs to take a walk," I said.

Beau looked over at Biscuit, snoring peacefully.

"I think he's asleep," he said.

I put a hand over my mouth to keep from smiling.

"It's been a while," I said.

He looked blankly at me a moment. "Good idea," he said. After getting to his feet, he held out a hand to help me up.

"Am I going?" I asked.

He grinned. "I was hoping you would."

I smiled back, biting my lip. "Come on Biscuit," I said, but kept my gaze on Beau's.

Biscuit stoood up and nuzzled my fingers, then Beau's.

"I think he's ready."

"Well," Beau said. "You aren't. I'll get your coat."

I scratched Biscuit's ears while Beau gathered up our winter garb.

As he held my coat for me to slide one arm in, then the next, I had an image.

I was wearing a red cocktail dress with matching stiletto heels. Instead of a cabin in the mountains, I was in a fancy hotel ballroom.

And the man holding my coat was not Beau. I didn't see the man's face, but I *knew* he was someone else.

It wasn't just that I had only just met Beau, it was something else. This man had a different *feel*.

Not wanting to think about anything else, I shoved the memory aside and focused on Beau as he buttoned the oversized coat, then tightened it with a belt. He handed me thick waterproof gloves that would most certainly not pass any fashion inspections in the city.

How long before he got tired of bundling me up to go outside in the snow?

I shoved that thought aside, too, as we stepped outside in the moonlight.

I followed Beau's gaze as he looked up at the mountaintops. Clouds were gathered around the peaks.

"It's going to snow again," I said.

"You can tell by the clouds?" he asked, looking at me with surprise.

"Yeah," I said with a little shrug. "Those are lenticular clouds."

. . .

"I'M IMPRESSED," he said.

"Why?"

He took my hands as we walked along, aimlessly following Biscuit.

"Not everyone knows much about the weather," he said. "Especially not a girl from Texas who hasn't spent much time in the mountains."

"Ah," I said. "but remember I'm a librarian, so I know a lot about a lot of things."

"Right," he said.

But librarians didn't wear fancy gowns to fancy cocktail parties.

Something wasn't adding up.

Maybe I was married to someone important. I touched my bare ring finger. I wasn't wearing a ring. Maybe I had been having an affair.

I stopped and shook my head.

If I was going to invent a past for myself, I should at least invent a good past, not a shady one.

I'd been traveling with a dog, for Goodness sakes. Surely that meant I was a good person.

"Penny for your thoughts," Beau said.

I smiled over at him, feeling the scowl between my brows relaxing. I squeezed his hand.

"I was just contemplating who I might be. You know. In my previous life."

"It's still your life," he said.

As we walked in silence, I told myself he was right and that it was normal for me to feel sad that this wasn't my real life.

"If you want it to be," Beau said.

My heart lightened just a bit. "What do you mean?"

"As someone with a past that I would prefer to forget, I think I can say with some conviction that it's okay to reinvent yourself and let the past go. At least I hope so."

"Is that what you're doing?"

"That's my plan. Yes."

I bit my lip as I considered.

Replayed the vague random memory of being at a fancy ball. Was that me? Or was this who I really was?

Maybe I was both. Some people had more than one facet to their personality. My Grandma Savannah was a good example. She had a place in the mountains and …

I froze. My feet refused to move.

I tried to block out the thought. But it was there.

"What's wrong?" Beau asked. "You remembered something."

"I think I have a grandmother named Savannah."

Beau took both my hands and looked directly into my eyes. "Does your grandmother have a last name?"

"I don't know," I said, looking away. "I don't want to think about it."

He swept a lock of hair off my cheek.

"It's okay to remember," he said. "It won't change what we have."

I nodded and started walking again.

I wanted to believe that, too.

But in my heart, I knew it wasn't true.

When I remembered who I was, everything was going to change.

20

BEAU

*B*iscuit took off after a chipmunk, then came rushing back toward us at lightning speed. Camila laughed and ducked behind me, but Biscuit skidded to a halt right next to her.

"He seems to be having a good time," I said.

It must be nice to be a dog and have no cares in the world.

Even though I told Camila that nothing was going to change once she figured out who she really was, I didn't believe it. I *wanted* to believe it. and I wanted her to believe it.

I wanted it to be true.

But I knew as clear as day that once her memory came back everything would change. She would go back to her life in Texas and I would be left here to figure what I wanted to do next.

It was a good problem to have, I suppose. Having steady retirement money coming in at such a young age. But the options were feeling too wide, at least at the moment.

I couldn't get my thoughts to settle.

Although I had planned on having months of isolation to

figure out just who I was outside of being an officer in the Air Force, that had not happened.

And I wouldn't change any of that for the world.

Having Camila here had derailed my thoughts. I did not want her to go.

"The cold air is refreshing," she said. "Don't you think?"

"Agreed." I pulled her close and kissed her on the cheek. "Thank you."

"You're welcome."

"So your grandmother's name is Savannah," I said. "Any other memories? Any images?"

She shook her head and kept her gaze straight ahead.

"When do you think they will have the electricity back on?" she asked, obviously changing the direction of the conversation.

"It could take weeks."

She looked at me a little stunned. "Seriously?"

"I don't have any way to report it and I doubt anyone will check."

"It's on some kind of electronic system, right? They should be able to see that it's out."

"You are a city girl," I said, teasingly. "But you know what, I really don't know how they're set up."

"Surely," she said, with a little shiver.

"Time to head back," I said, sweeping her about in the other direction.

Camila was being quiet. I had a feeling this had something to do with her memory.

If she remembered her grandmother's name, it most likely meant she was starting to remember things.

Yet she was fighting it.

I should be happy that she was getting her memory back.

But I wasn't.

I dreaded the hour that was sure to come.

21

CAMILA

*W*hen I woke, it was still dark.

The fire had burned low, so I knew Beau was fast asleep.

It wasn't so quiet as it had been when I woke up the morning of the storm.

A wolf or a dog or whatever it was howled in the distance and couple of minutes later, another one answered.

I didn't move. I just stared at the flames as they greedily licked up the wood. The scent of wood smoke was strong. Not clean and odorless like the gas flames I was accustomed to.

I wasn't cold. Not on the surface anyway.

My name is Camila Worthington. The daughter of Quinn Worthington. The granddaughter of Noah Worthington— owner and founder of Skye Travels. A self-made billionaire.

I'm an airplane pilot. Small jets. Not commercial.

The worst thing. Biscuit wasn't even my dog. He belonged to a fifteen-year-old blind girl named Amy.

The truth fell over me like a ton of bricks.

It was a bit hard for me to breath.

I forced myself to take a deep breath, but the air came in cold, piercing my lungs like shards of glass.

But I was shivering. Biscuit came over, licked my face, then yipped.

His bark woke Beau immediately.

"What's wrong?" he asked.

Biscuit was licking my face again.

"Camila," Beau said. "What's wrong?"

He got up and threw some logs into the fire. Poked at them to get the fire roaring.

Then he gathered me up in his arms.

"Camila." He moved closer to the fire, taking me with him.

I couldn't get close enough to him. But I was tired. So tired.

"My name is Camila Worthington," I said, but I wasn't sure if Beau heard me.

"I know," he said. "I know. You're okay. You're going to be okay."

I nodded against his chest. Yes. I would be okay.

But my mind was racing with images of a full and busy life that had been beyond my reach until tonight.

"Focus on your breathing," Beau said, one hand wrapped around my waist, the other tangled in my hair. "Focus on my voice. You're going to be okay. Don't try to fight these feelings. Just ride it out. It will pass."

I don't know how long we sat like that, him talking me through the panic attack.

But I began to settle and the shivering slowed.

Then I did as he said and closed my eyes. Let my mind go blank. Focusing only on the sound of his voice.

The moment I had been dreading had come.

22

BEAU

*T*he ambulance ride to Denver was the longest hour of my life.

The sway of the ambulance. The roar of the tires on the highway. After being in the cabin for days, it was a shock to my system.

They gave Camila a sedative and intravenous fluid, so I simply sat there watching her. Watching her chest move up and down with each breath. Watching her steady heart rate on the monitor.

The paramedics gave up on trying to get me to talk. I'm not even sure they had asked how I was related to her. They would have had to give me a tranquilizer to get me away from her and I'm sure they knew that.

But once the ambulance arrived at the hospital, everything moved rapidly.

Not only had word traveled fast once I reported that I had Camila Worthington, alive and well, but apparently her family —what looked like a whole tribe of people—were already gathered in Denver.

The thought crossed my mind that the whole Skye Travels

company must have closed their doors from the looks of things. But, of course, I'm sure they had employees to keep things running.

At any rate, not one person so much as acknowledged me as Camila was swept inside and enveloped by at least two dozen relatives. Grandparents, parents, siblings, aunts, uncles, cousins. I don't think anyone even saw me.

Exhausted beyond words, I found a seat not far from the waiting room, close enough that I could keep an eye out for the doctors. To hear any report.

I just needed to know that she was going to be okay.

Everything else, I would deal with later.

But she had to be okay first.

I made myself a coffee, stood at the tall floor to ceiling window, and watched the sunset. How had that much time passed?

It seemed like just minutes when I had woken to her labored breathing. Thank God for Biscuit.

I wasn't sure I would have woke up if the dog hadn't barked.

I faded into the background. I listened. I learned.

Camila, as I had suspected, had gotten a light case of hypothermia. I blamed myself for that. I'd neglected the fire, sleeping deeply as it burned down.

The hypothermia coupled with the jolt of getting her memory back had sent her into shock.

She was going to be okay. They were, in fact, sending her home tomorrow. Not home to Texas, but home to her Aunt Madison's house here in Denver.

Camila had been traveling alone, delivering Biscuit to a young blind girl. So it wasn't just chance that Biscuit had watched out for Camila. He was a well-trained dog. I did not know how Camila was going to take finding out that Biscuit was not, in fact, her dog. The two of them had developed quite a bond with what they had gone through together.

Camila had been trying to get ahead of the storm, but it had come in earlier than expected.

None of this was particularly unexpected or anything that she and I could not get past.

What turned out to be troubling was that she had a boyfriend.

His name was Todd and he was also a pilot. I was unclear on whether they were engaged or pre-engaged.

Whichever it was, it seemed like they had been together for a while and Todd had been accepted into the family.

So... I sipped my coffee and decided that I would slip out, take an Uber back to Whiskey Springs, and maybe go back to the cabin. Maybe not.

Maybe I would find another way... another place... to come up with my new direction for my future. Probably not the cabin. The cabin was contaminated now.

Just the thought of going back there made me sick to my stomach.

I tossed my empty coffee cup into the wastebasket and headed out into the night.

Putting Camila, my angel, behind me.

PART II

23

CAMILA

*I*t had been three months, almost to the day, since my plane crash.

Mid-December, full on Christmas season.

The fireworks over Uptown had been spectacular. The red and green lights all along Post Oak were perfectly synchronized and the tree in the Galleria was as grand as it always was.

The lights twinkled along with the Christmas music blasting over the speakers.

I tucked my hands into my light blue wool coat—I never seemed to be able to get warm enough anymore—and watched my six-year-old niece make a perfect axel jump. Her skates sliced into the ice, enveloping her in a magical sparkle lasting only a second.

Sophia was the only girl on the ice. Two other girls, older, probably eight or nine, had come in and were giggling at something as they laced their skates on.

Nothing like Sophia. I know she enjoyed skating, but she took it seriously. And she never skated with friends. As far as I knew, she didn't even have any friends, but that was another matter. Neither did I for the most part.

Otherwise the Galleria was deserted. It had taken some pull to get Sophia scheduled on the ice this early in the morning. Six o'clock was usually the earliest they let anyone in. Sophia had started skating nearly an hour ago at five.

Since Sophia came to the ice rink every morning, someone had to bring her. Driven as she was, it took a village to get her here. I had volunteered. I liked the routine of it. The uniqueness.

I'd heard some talk that Sophia's parents were considering building a new home, right here in Houston, with a private ice rink right in the middle of it.

There was no doubt that Sophia was on an Olympic bound track. She would rather ice-skate than anything. Dolls? No. Computer games? No way. Dress up? Only if it involved a skating dress.

Personally, I thought she was still young and only time would tell if she would tire of the sport. But everyone else seemed certain that her laser-focused passion was leading her on a straight-path to the Olympics.

I had to admit, she reminded me of myself once I'd started solo flying. It was like an addiction that I couldn't tame.

But for these three months, the only time I had been on an airplane had been when Grandpa Noah had flown me back to Houston after the doctors had given me permission to even board an airplane.

Although my request for my grandfather to be the one to fly me home had set off a wave of grumblings, I did not care. He was the one person I trusted completely. The best pilot in existence as far as I was concerned.

There were so many others who wanted what they seemed to see as the privilege of getting me home. My older brother. My twin brother.

My boyfriend.

The music changed to a romantic, happy tune that used to bring me joy. Now it just made me sad.

Despite the festiveness of the season, I had no joy for it in me.

If I had to describe the way I felt, I was quite simply numb.

The few days I had spent in the cabin with Beau haunted me.

Contrary to what I had feared, I had not forgotten him. But I think it might have been easier if I had.

I even missed the dog.

That was funny because I had a silver Persian cat named Kit Kat that I loved dearly.

But nonetheless, Biscuit and I, having been through the trauma of a plane crash in the dark mountains together, had bonded.

I could visit, but that would require flying and I wasn't released yet. If I couldn't fly myself, I wasn't going.

I was doing what I was supposed to do to get insurance to release me back into the cockpit.

Including therapy twice a week. I honestly think I would have been better off healing at my own pace in my own way rather than with the artificial healing that came with therapy.

But it was a requirement, so I did it.

Much like Sophia, I was driven. Even with this setback, I was still driven.

When the time came for me to get back in the cockpit, I wasn't sure how I would feel, but I hoped that it would bring some of the joy back to my spirit.

And even though I hoped it would, I had a feeling that without Beau, there was very little that could bring me true happiness, at least for the moment.

I clapped for my niece and smiled.

But the smile was not real. My therapist had said to go through the motions.

Fake it 'til you make it.

So I was faking my way through the holiday season one day at the time.

And somehow I knew I would learn how to live without Beau.

Somehow being in that crash. Surviving. Being rescued by Beau. Had opened up a new compartment in my head.

I had discovered an affinity for dogs, at least big, gangly labs.

I had learned that my vegetarian self liked bacon.

And, most significant of all, I had discovered that my relationship with Todd had continued simply because I had not bothered to end it. It had been too easy to just let it coast.

Until I had lost my memory long enough to fall in love with Beau.

I had to end my relationship with Todd. I had not done it yet, but I knew that I had to.

As far as Beau went, I didn't know how to find him. Other than a vague notion that it was somewhere outside of Whiskey Springs, Colorado, I did not know where the cabin was.

And I did not know Beau's last name.

The two girls came out and skated around Sophia. She wasn't the least bit fazed.

She was like a movie star.

My aunt was going to need that house with the private ice rink.

24

BEAU

I think I picked Houston because of Camila.

In fact, if I was honest with myself, I *know* I picked Houston because of Camila.

The traffic was the worst, but this time of day, before the morning rush hour, it was tolerable and it was easy to forget how bad it would get before long. Bumper to bumper. Horns honking. People panhandling on the street corners. The scent of exhaust perfuming the air.

Houston was most definitely an all-American city in an all-American state.

I could get behind that.

With or without Camila.

I knew I could find her. Her grandfather, Noah Worthington owned Skye Travels and Worthington Enterprises. I even knew *where* to find her. Well, not her specifically, but her grandfather and that would point me to her.

As a matter of fact, I could probably walk up to the Skye Travels terminal today and find her. I had to remind myself that Camila was a pilot.

I just kept picturing her walking through the woods, snow falling all around her.

I turned on the blinker and pulled into the left turn lane to head into the Galleria. Cars stopped and waited for us to cross the traffic. I didn't have the siren on, just the lights. I only used the siren when absolutely necessary.

The current crisis. A six-year-old female with a fall injury.

After parking in front of the door of the Galleria, my coworker and I grabbed our gear and headed inside.

Foregoing my winter of self-reflection, I fell back on my foundation. I applied for a paramedic position.

I sent in literally one application and immediately landed the job.

Sounded as much like it was meant to be as anything, so I made a road trip to Houston. Could have flown, but I took those three days on the road in lieu of three months in the cabin.

Still didn't have anything resolved.

It was going to take me a while to let Camila go. She was the one I had been looking for when I hadn't even known I was looking.

Even at this time of the morning, there was a crowd gathered around the injured girl. Injury always drew a crowd in public places. People had an innate need to see that there were others worse off than they were.

I kept my jaded opinion to myself, of course. Part of my job was to provide optimism. People in a crisis needed to know that they were going to be okay. Those around them needed that optimism, too.

The first thing I saw was a young lady kneeling on the cold ice. The young lady was wearing a light blue wool coat, but she was wearing a flowy dress and sneakers. The new style that baffled and intrigued me. Reminded me of that special casual time at the end of a date when a girl took off her heels and threw on a pair of sneakers to run a quick errand.

She had to be freezing cold, kneeling there like that.

The next thing I saw was a little girl wearing a sequined emerald green skating dress.

After my training and years working with soldiers, I was still getting used to seeing injured civilians, especially women and children.

Cradling one arm with the other, the child leaned against the young lady.

The child was first to see us coming toward them. I saw the hope light up in her eyes. She said something to the young lady.

They whispered for a minute, then the child lifted her head and looked at me.

My gaze trained on the injured girl, I gazed into emerald green eyes that reflected the deep green of her dress.

Her eyes were bathed with moisture, but there something about her eyes… the way she looked… that gave me a start.

There was something vaguely familiar.

I shook it off.

When I'd moved to Houston, I had expected to see Camila everywhere and my unconscious brain had not failed me.

"Sophia," I said. "My name is Beau. Can I take a look at what hurts?"

As the little girl nodded, it registered somewhere in the back of my mind that the young lady in the light blue wool coat froze. I think I felt it more than saw it.

Maybe it was something about the way she smelled. Or the way she sat crouched on the ice, unconcerned for herself.

Whatever it was, I still was not prepared for the jolt of recognition that hit me when I turned and saw Camila kneeling there.

Everything seemed to slow down almost going into slow motion.

I saw the recognition reflected in her own eyes. Saw the jolt of surprise shadowed by doubt.

While my system absorbed the realization that I had found Camila, I examined the little girl's shoulder.

It wasn't broken. With the moves these girls did on skates, I figured she was lucky.

Not that she was feeling very lucky right now.

"It's not broken," I told her.

Sophia looked up at me with big green eyes full of gratitude as my colleague wrapped a warm wool blanket around her.

Camila pulled her gaze from mine to focus on Sophia again.

"You're a brave girl," Camila said. "You're going to be okay."

Sophia nodded. The little girl really did look quite brave.

"We're going to take her in for x-rays anyway," I said. "just to make sure. Get her fixed up to make sure she heals properly."

An accident like this could dash a young girl's dreams. My heart went out to Sophia. I knew she would always remember this day when she'd crashed onto the ice.

But hopefully she would move past it, none the worse for wear. The alternative was crushed dreams hooked onto the traumatic event.

I hooked a pulse oximeter to one of her little fingers and again, my gaze met Camila's.

For a split second, I imagined that Sophia could be our child. We could have a beautiful child like this together.

Then I remembered. Camila had someone already.

I had not known that she already had a child. How could I know? I did not stalk people on social media. I didn't even have an account. There was nothing in my life that I wanted to broadcast on the billboard of the Internet.

At any rate, I had no right to be thinking about such things as children with regards to Camila.

After my colleague and I slid Sophia onto the stretcher, I

held out a hand to help up the woman who had hijacked my brain for the last three months. Her hands were cold. I grabbed one of the extra blankets off the stretcher and wrapped it around her shoulders.

"Thank you," she said, her teeth chattering with cold.

And suddenly it was three months ago and Angel was freezing again.

But it wasn't three months ago.

And her name wasn't Angel.

25

CAMILA

I strode beside the stretcher, holding Sophia's hand. My niece was putting on a brave face.

I could only imagine that she must be terrified.

The pirouette had been perfectly executed. But when her skates hit the ice, she didn't stop twirling.

She hit the ice with such a loud crash, that I thought I had heard the entire sheet of ice shatter.

I wasn't the one who had called for help.

Without even thinking, I had rushed around the barrier, down the steps, and out onto the ice.

I would never know how I had managed to cross several yards of ice to get to Sophia without falling down and breaking something myself, but I had managed it.

My heart slammed hard as I caught my first sight of the flashing ambulance lights. I hated that this had happened to Sophia, worse especially that it happened on my watch.

My hands trembled as I pulled my cell out of my handbag.

I needed to call my aunt. Sophia's mother.

"Where are you taking her," I asked.

"Methodist," one of the paramedics said.

"Which one?" I asked impatiently.

"Downtown."

I dialed my aunt's number. Held the phone up to Sophia's cheek.

"Tell Mommy you're okay," I said, swallowing the lump in my throat.

"Hi Mommy," Sophia said. "I'm going to ride in an ambulance."

I cringed. Not the way to start a phone conversation.

Then and only then did I allow my gaze to shift back to Beau.

He was in deep concentration, monitoring Sophia's vitals. I took a deep ragged breath. That was why I trusted him. He was good at what he did.

I trusted him with my niece's life, just as he had saved mine.

There would be time to talk with him later. To find out how he ended up here in Houston. To thank him for rescuing me from the plane crash and being so kind.

There was more, of course. So much more.

As I climbed into the back of the ambulance to sit next to Sophia, I watched Beau's competent movements as he settled her in for the ride.

I was reminded that he hadn't looked for me. He knew who I was. I wasn't that hard to find.

He would have his reasons, of course.

Then again, he was in Houston.

As far as I knew, he was supposed to still be in the cabin in the mountains. He had said he was going to spend the winter there.

But here he was.

The thought tapped a lightness in my heart that I hadn't felt for three months.

"Are you going to turn on the siren?" Sophia asked one of the paramedics.

I smiled at Sophia. She did not look terrified. She looked like she was having an adventure.

The resilience of a six-year-old girl was enviable.

The smile still on my lips, my gaze flicked up to Beau.

And he smiled back.

It was brief. Brief, but meaningful. I saw it in his eyes. We had a history.

And in that simple gaze, I felt that shared meaningfulness.

As the ambulance pulled out of the parking lot and headed downtown, it was still dark enough that the festive Christmas tree lights blinked through their sequence of blue and green and red and gold.

It was as though I was seeing the lights for the first time this season.

They were beautiful.

26

BEAU

*T*he distraction of a woman had been the downfall of many men.

Right now, I had a job to do.

This child was not Camila's. *Tell Mommy you're okay.*

With those words, relief had flooded through me. Maybe I wasn't so far off base after all. But I kept my focus on my driving.

Whoever this child was to Camila, I didn't want her having long-term negative effects of this accident because of something I did or did not do. I was the one responsible for Sophia right now.

Once she was safely passed off to the hospital staff, then and only then would I allow myself to think about Camila.

I stopped at a red light, looked back, but I couldn't see Camila.

The drive to the hospital took forever. Even after I pulled in and secured the vehicle, my work was not over.

Somehow I was the one standing there to help Camila to the ground.

I started to take her hand, then just gave my head a quick shake before I put both my hands on her waist and swung her easily to her feet.

I left my hands there for only an extra second, but it was long enough for her to look up at me. For me to see that she wasn't shivering. Finally. I'd had enough of her shivering to last a lifetime.

And her eyes. Her big green eyes were full of questions.

Then they were wheeling Sophia inside and Camila pulled away to go with her.

I didn't have to go inside, but I would.

Before closing the door, I noticed that I had a last name for Sophia now. Worthington.

Of course.

The little girl must be Camila's niece.

That explained the obvious affection between them and told me that I hadn't actually imagined the resemblance between them.

I went inside, calm and cool on the outside, a bundle of nerves on the inside.

She remembered me. I saw it in her eyes. That didn't mean that she wanted to remember me, much less see me.

But fate had gotten us this far and I wasn't one to spit in fate's face. On the contrary. This was the kind of stuff a person couldn't make up. It had to mean something.

By the time I got inside, they were already taking Sophia to a room. The Worthington name no doubt opened doors everywhere. Even the hospital.

The thought slowed my steps.

I was an Air Force veteran. Not a rich man of society.

Camila was out of my league.

I didn't normally care about such things. But a Worthington was a whole other level than where I was or ever would be.

I would talk to her, but I needn't have any kind of expectations.

Back in the cabin, she hadn't known who she was, much less who I was. Now that she was back home...

I shut my thoughts down right there and went in search of a cup of coffee.

27

CAMILA

"How did you get here so quick?" I asked my Aunt Ainsley.

"I was in the area." Ainsley shrugged. "Has the doctor been in yet?"

"Just x-rays," I said.

Ainsley ran a hand lightly over the bandage on Sophia's shoulder. "It's probably just scuffed," she said. "How did this happen, Sweetie?"

Sophia's lip trembled for the first time since the accident and she lowered her head.

"It was an accident," I said, coming to Sophia's rescue. "It was a perfect pirouette, but the ice was just too… slick."

Ainsley shot me a look, but she pulled Sophia toward her. "It's okay," she said. "It wasn't your fault."

"We probably overreacted," I said. Seeing Sophia fall and go sliding across the ice, shoulder first, had frozen my heart.

It didn't help that it gave me a flashback to the plane crash.

"It's okay," Ainsley said again. "We're all still a little jumpy, I guess."

I blew out a breath. At least Ainsley understood. My whole family was very understanding.

A few minutes later, the physician came in and confirmed that Sophia was going to be just fine.

His recommendation that Sophia take a week off from ice skating, however, was met with outright opposition that could only come from a six-year-old girl.

"I'll just step out," I said, not wanting to get in the middle of how Ainsley resolved this particular issue with her child.

Besides, I had to confess that I wanted to see if Beau was still out there. Surely he wouldn't just leave without at least talking to me.

Feeling a bit nervous, I stopped by the restroom and took a quick inventory of my appearance.

My skirt, a thin flowy cotton was dry, but there was a rip near my right knee. My hair was okay, nothing a quick brush couldn't fix. I dabbed on some glossy lipstick and deemed myself presentable.

I went down the hallway and made my way to the door. I stepped out.

Midmorning now, it was still cold, but the sun was bright. A gust of wind caught my skirt and tossed my hair into my face.

The ambulance was gone.

Beau had left without seeing me.

My heart shattered.

I understood. He was working. Could have gotten called out on another call.

It wasn't all about me.

Besides, I reminded myself, he had known where to find me and he hadn't bothered.

Just leave it alone.

I took a deep breath, turned and went back inside. It was certainly too cold to stand outside. Any inkling of fondness I might have had for cold weather had vanished. I could just flat out do without it.

I went back inside.

I didn't even have my car. I could call an Uber or catch a ride with Ainsley. But since Ainsley lived in a different direction from me, I decided the Uber would be the better choice. Besides, I didn't want to get in the middle of her and Sophia's ban from the ice rink.

"Hello Angel."

My heart nearly jumped out of my chest and I nearly dropped my phone.

Beau was standing there grinning at me.

"Hi," I said, sliding my phone back into my purse. "What are you doing here? The ambu—"

"I took the rest of the day off. I needed to see you."

"Oh," I said, tucking my hair behind my ears. "I was just looking for you."

"Do you have time to..." he stopped, glanced toward another hallway. "grab a coffee? They said there's a Starbucks on the fourth floor."

"Sure," I said. "I just need to text my sister."

"Go ahead," he said and we started walking toward the elevator.

ME: *Do you need me to stay?*

We stepped onto the elevator and I studied Beau out of the corner of my eyes. When we were at the cabin, I hadn't realized that Beau was a full head taller than me. He looked good in his uniform, too.

AUNT AINSLEY: *No. We're about to leave. Do you need a ride?*

ME: *Grabbing an Uber. But thanks.*

My family worried about me. It was a good problem to have, I suppose.

We stepped off the elevator into another lobby. This one opened up for a view of the lobby on the ground floor. A big cheerful Christmas tree stood in one corner, piles of cheerfully wrapped gifts piled beneath it.

"Is Sophia good?" he asked.

"I think we overreacted," I said. "Seeing her twirling in the air, then falling like that…"

"Yeah. I can only imagine. It's amazing what those youngsters can do."

"And she's only six years old," I said. "And already better than anyone else out there."

We ordered our coffees and sat on a bench with a view of downtown.

"It's a whole different view," he said.

I knew what he meant. He was comparing the view of downtown Houston to the view of the stunning Rocky Mountains.

"Both are stunning in their own way," I decided.

"Agreed."

"So…" I took a sip of my hot coffee. "You aren't there."

He smiled sheepishly. "My heart wasn't in it anymore."

"So you came here," I said, holding my warm cup in both hands.

"You're here."

"But… you… didn't… tell me…"

"Maybe I was working up the courage."

"I see," I said. But I didn't think I believed him. "I didn't know how to find you. To thank you."

"You didn't have to thank me," he said, serious now.

"I'd like to anyway."

"Seeing you again, healthy and well, is thanks enough."

He leaned forward, looking into my eyes. His eyes were so blue. Like the sky in the most beautiful of summer days.

"You're confusing me a little bit," I said. "but my therapist warned me to expect that."

"You're in therapy," he said.

"It's not so bad," I said, but I hadn't meant to tell him that.

Seeing him, looking into his eyes was like a shock to my system. I had thought about this man every day. Dreamed about him at night. Tried unsuccessfully to keep him out of my therapy sessions. The psychologist put two and two together. Plane crash. Rescued. Stranded in a snow storm.

But sitting here. Talking to him. Knowing I had yet to break up with Todd.

I wasn't sure how to go forward.

28

BEAU

*C*amila seemed nervous.

And she looked more fragile now than she had in the cabin.

I had no way of knowing what she had been through over the past three months. And although I probably shouldn't, I felt guilty for not being here for her.

I wanted to smooth the concern away from between her brows. That or distract her away from wherever this conversation was taking her.

Since I didn't know where she stood, I opted for the latter.

"Won any Blackjack games lately?" I asked.

That got me the smile I was looking for.

"Actually, yes," she said.

"So I was wrong?" I asked, teasing her. "You're a dealer on the side?"

"No. I'm not a dealer." She rolled her eyes. "But my brothers and my boy… twin like to play on family night."

"Ah," I said. "So it's a family thing." She almost said boyfriend. I had so been hoping I had gotten that wrong. There were two ways to go with this. I went the safe way. "You have a twin?"

"I do." She smiled. "His name is Conner."

"Camila and Conner," I said. "Cute. Family names?"

"Not at all. I don't know where my family comes up with their names."

"I think you're fortunate," I said. "I come from a long line of Beaus."

She laughed. "You're kidding, right?"

"I wish I was kidding."

She looked at me with those big green eyes. "So you're like Beau the third or something?"

"No," I said with a little shake of my head. "It's not that bad. They change it up. My father was Wilford Beau and I'm Beau Wilford."

She put a hand over her mouth. "That's kinda cute."

"Cute," I said, feigning offense.

She just grinned.

It occurred to me then that we were sitting in a hospital drinking coffee when we could and very well should be somewhere else.

"You rode in the ambulance," I said, stating the obvious.

"So did you."

"So we're stranded here in the hospital."

She straightened. "I was about to call an Uber."

"Right." I was not ready for her to go. "Can I buy you lunch?"

"Okay," she said. "As long as you don't mind being seen with a girl wearing a ripped skirt."

I scoffed. "Are you kidding? You do know that's the new style, right?"

"It is not," she said.

"It is now," I said, with a little wink.

She shook her head.

"Tell me you don't own a pair of jeans with a rip at the knee."

She started to answer, but her phone chimed. She glanced at it, bringing the little frown back between her brows.

"Need to take that?" I asked.

She didn't answer, but she lowered the phone. "It's Todd," she said on a sigh.

"Who's Todd?" I asked, but I really, really did not want to hear the answer because I already knew.

"He's the guy who wants to marry me."

That was more information than I had expected. She wasn't supposed to tell me this, was she? Most girls didn't tell a guy they were interested in about another guy. Did that mean I was in the friend zone?

"Do you want to marry him?"

"No," she said, but she looked down at her phone. "It's just sort of… expected."

"How so?"

"His father and my father are friends, sort of, and Todd and I have known each other forever." She said it all on one long breath.

"Sounds complicated," I said.

"Yeah."

"Come on," I said. "Let's get out of here."

This was feeling more and more like a first date and I didn't really want it to be in a hospital. She and I had done more than our share of medical related activities.

29

CAMILA

*B*eau and I ended up at the Galleria.

I'd had to pick a place to go and since my car was still there, it seemed like the most logical place to go.

He held my hand in the back seat of the Uber. It was intimate and unexpected.

Memories of kisses in front of the fireplace.

When I had kissed Beau—three months ago, I had not known who I was. I hadn't known about Todd.

So now, oddly enough, being with Beau did not feel like cheating on Todd. In fact, the couple of times Todd had kissed me since the accident had felt like cheating on Beau.

The Galleria was crowded now. The huge Christmas tree planted right there on the ice rink was the same, but otherwise, the scene was completely different from that morning before the mall stores opened.

Christmas music playing in the background was barely audible over the voices.

There was no sign of Sophia's accident on the ice, of course. At least two dozen children and teens, with all levels of skill, glided around the rink, some not so much gliding as pulling themselves around the rink.

"Do you skate?" Beau asked as we looked over the railing at the skaters below.

"No," I said. "Maybe. I took lessons when I was a kid, but it just something that was sort of expected. My brothers were actually better than I was."

"Expected of them, too?"

"My parents had us take lessons for just about everything for at least a year. Ice skating. Horseback riding. Piano. The basics."

"Sounds grueling."

"They didn't want us to miss anything we might have an affinity for." I turned my attention to Beau. "What about you?"

"High school football. That's about it."

"I threw a few footballs," I said. "But never any training."

"You? Footballs?" I turned, leaning against the rail to look at her.

"Five brothers," I said.

He shrugged and changed the subject. "Did anything take? Besides aviation?"

"You mean am I good at anything else?"

"Are you?" There was a slight challenge in his expression.

"Well, I'm good at everything," I said. "But not everything brings me joy."

He laughed. "I understand. I think."

"Do you watch real football?"

"Been known to," he said.

I smiled at his diplomatic response. "Houston has a pretty good team, you know?"

"I'm aware," he said. "Look at those guys on the ice." He pointed at three guys, young teens on the ice now, skating around without a care in the world.

"Training for hockey," I said, then looked at him from beneath my lashes. "You want to give it a whirl?"

"Give what a whirl?" he asked.

"Ice skating."

"Wait a minute. I thought you were trying to talk me into taking you to a football game."

I laughed and grabbed his hand. "We can do that later."

I pulled him toward the rink entrance.

"At least I get a military discount to lessen my humiliation," he said when we reached the desk.

"We don't have to pay," I said. "I have a pass."

We checked out skates and sat on one of the benches while we laced up.

"This might not be a good idea," he said. "I've never done this."

I stood up. Checked his laces.

"Don't worry," I said. "I'll show you what to do."

I hadn't planned on getting back on the ice today, especially after Sophia's tumble, but I needed to do it for myself more than anything else.

I needed to get back on the horse. I was afraid that if I didn't, I never would.

And the way I saw it, it put me one step closer to getting back in the cockpit of an airplane.

30

BEAU

*T*here were some things a grown man shouldn't do.

Especially if he'd never done it before.

I was certain my feet were going to slide out from beneath me at any minute and I'd bust my ass.

But Camila turned out to be quite the instructor.

"You're a fast learner," she said. "Look at you."

She was right. I was skating. And on the surface, I was pretty sure my knees weren't wobbling.

I still didn't think it was a smart idea. There were so many bones that could be broken. And it did not help that I could name every one of them.

I was surprised that Camila was out on the ice after today's incident.

As I studied the determined set of her jaw, it occurred to me that she might have her own reasons that had nothing to do with me.

The three teenage boys zipped past us.

"Boys are fearless," she said.

"I'm beginning to think you are," I said.

She grinned and took my hand.

"We're holding up traffic," she said.

"You like speed, don't you?" I asked as she pulled me along.

"Maybe I like getting where I'm going fast," she said.

During my training, I had jumped out of airplanes. I had even trained on water and ice, but there was something different about this gliding around the rink. No protective gear. People watching.

Then I slipped. Not paying attention. But Camila grabbed my arm and steadied me.

With my arms around her, I looked down into her emerald green eyes.

"Lunch?" I asked, distracting myself from kissing her right there on the ice.

"Good idea."

A few minutes later we sat at a café near the skating rink. Though we could still see the ice rink from here, we sat inside the café. I much preferred the view from here.

At least sitting across from Camila, I could focus on her.

Her cheeks were flushed prettily from the exertion.

After we ordered, I reached across the table and put my hand on hers.

"How have you been?" I asked.

She shrugged, but turned her hand over so our palms were touching. "Surviving."

"Same here," I said, then sat forward. "Look. At the hospital. Your family was there. And I didn't want to intrude."

"It's okay," she said, but her eyes were moist. "I understand."

"I didn't want to... confuse you."

"You wouldn't. But I don't fault you for leaving. My family can be overwhelming."

"I thought about you." I stopped. Cleared my throat.

"I thought about you, too," I said. "But I didn't know how to find you."

"I guess I hadn't quite figured out what to do about you yet," I admitted.

The server brought our food. A burger for me and a veggie burger for her.

"You don't eat meat," I said.

She smiled. "No. But it seems I have an affinity for bacon."

I laughed. "Who doesn't?"

"Don't tell anyone," she said as she bit into a French fry.

"Your secret is safe with me," I said.

Her phone chimed again. Same ring tone as before. She didn't look at it.

"You need to get that?"

"It's Todd," she said.

"You should talk to him."

"I know." She looked across to the skating rink. "I just don't want to."

I really didn't know what to say to that. So we ate in silence for a few minutes.

"I really liked Biscuit," she said, looking at me again.

"I know. He really liked you, too."

"Guess what?" She grinned. "I have a cat."

All I could do was laugh. Camila was absolutely charming. And the thing is. She didn't even know it.

If only she didn't have a boyfriend...

31

CAMILA

*B*eating the rush hour traffic, I pulled into my garage and turned off the motor.

I sat for a few minutes waiting while the garage door lumbered down.

My day had been far, far more eventful than I had expected when I left home this morning.

Just like it had three months ago.

The plane crash had taught me that nothing was guaranteed. That every day was a gift.

It was an unusual perspective for a twenty-six-year old, but it was what I had.

I went inside my townhouse and dropped my keys and purse on the table by the door. I slipped my phone into my pocket.

Kit Kat ran down the stairs, meowing for me.

I grabbed her up and stroked her silky fur. She purred like a freight train.

"Hungry?" I asked.

She nuzzled my cheek.

Going into the kitchen, I put Kit Kat on the counter and opened a can of her favorite tuna favored cat food.

I took a bottle of water from the refrigerator and sat at the bar to watch her eat.

"What should I do, Kit Kat?" I asked.

Kit Kat didn't answer, of course. I should probably ask one of my aunts. Aunt Ainsley would know. Or Aunt Brianna. Aunt Brianna was the coolest of my four aunts.

I should definitely talk to her. I just wasn't ready to.

My whole family expected me to marry Todd. We had been a couple forever.

They would not understand how I had managed to fall in love with someone else. And in such a short amount of time. While I did not even know who I was.

Besides, Beau had not said anything about seeing each other again.

I didn't have his phone number and he didn't have mine.

I plucked a white daisy from the vase in front of me and toyed with its petals.

Well hell.

I blew out a breath.

Kit Kat lifted her head and glanced at me, then went back to eating.

So basically Beau and I had had two chance encounters. And we had managed to not share contact information either time.

I had thought about it, but I'd been waiting for him to make the first move.

My brain was still foggy from the concussion and the hypothermia, so I could have misread his interest.

It wasn't like I had a lot of experience in that department. Todd was the only boy I had ever dated.

I slipped the daisy back into the vase and leaned my elbows on the counter.

I *had* told Beau that I had a boyfriend. Probably a stupid thing to do.

It made sense that he was waiting for me to say something about getting together again first.

I'd missed that one. It had gone right by me.

I definitely needed to talk to Aunt Brianna.

Pulling my phone out of my pocket I sent a quick text.

ME: *Are you busy?*

Thought bubbles. I put away Kit Kat's empty plate. She jumped down and scurried to finish her afternoon nap.

I went in my living, got comfortable on the couch and considering taking a nap myself.

Aunt Brianna was always doing something. Always busy. But she was always willing to drop everything when someone needed her help. Everybody in my family was, but Aunt Brianna was the only one who wasn't a psychologist or a pilot.

I didn't want to talk about flying right now and it invariably came up anytime I talked with Aunt Ainsley.

As for my other aunts, all psychologists, they would all just want to get into my head. To try to check on my mental health status.

BRIANNA: *Need me to come over?*

God, I loved Aunt Brianna. She was THE best aunt a girl could have.

BRIANNA: *Let me just finish up one thing and I'll be over.*

BRIANNA: *Are you home?*

ME: *Yes.*

She had no doubt heard about Sophia's wreck on the ice by now. She probably thought that was what I wanted to talk about.

Well. She was going to be surprised.

It occurred to me then to check my voicemail.

Todd had called three times and left three messages. Why wouldn't he learn to text?

The first two times he called, he just hung up. The third time, he left a message. I could tell from the background noise that he was on an airplane.

"See you tonight," he said.

I set my phone on the coffee table and closed my eyes.

Tonight was the night then.

I had to tell him.

It was becoming evidently clear to me that I was not in love with Todd and I wasn't sure I ever really was.

Not like I was with Beau.

32

BEAU

*H*ow had I let that happen?
Again?

I'd let Camila just drive away without getting her number or giving her mine.

The hours we'd spent together had reaffirmed the way I felt about her. It was more than just a passing thing.

I stripped down and stepped into the shower.

Just stood there, letting the hot water cascade over my head.

It was complicated.

She had a boyfriend.

It wasn't my place to come between her and her long-time boyfriend. Todd.

But she said she did not want to marry him.

Still. Family pressure could be overwhelming.

I knew people, male and female, who had married people they really didn't want to marry just because it was expected of them.

Worst of all was after the wedding plans started. Wedding plans were like a freight train that once it picked up speed, it couldn't be stopped.

I didn't know if Camila had wedding plans yet or not. If she did, I was doomed. If she didn't then maybe, just maybe, I had a chance.

Stepping out of the shower, I toweled off and threw on a pair of sweatpants and a t-shirt.

I didn't have any friends. I preferred to stay to myself. Any friends I had were military buddies. I knew where they were. Could have called any of them.

But I preferred to keep my personal life separate from my work life.

I went to the kitchen and grabbed a beer, twisted the lid off.

Maybe I should get a dog. Then at least, I'd have an excuse to take a walk around the apartment complex without looking like a creep.

I missed Biscuit, too. I even knew where they had delivered him. Had the girl's phone number. Had talked to her. She had actually called to thank me.

But she was a child. I didn't feel comfortable calling her even to check on Biscuit.

I stretched out on the couch and flipped on the television. At least I had Netflix to keep me company.

When my phone chimed I picked it up and scowled at the caller id. It was Lucy, a coworker.

I didn't answer. I let voicemail pick up.

But Lucy turned around and sent me a text.

LUCY: *Heard you took the rest of the day off. Hope you're feeling ok.*

ME: *Had some personal things to do.*

LUCY: *Great! Want to grab a beer?*

I stared at the beer in my hand. I already had a beer.

Lucy had been a bit flirty in retrospect, but I hadn't paid any attention to it.

Here was my chance to make a friend.

But I had a feeling Lucy was wanting to be more than a friend.

She was a coworker, so I couldn't just ignore her. I had to give her an answer.

My fingers hovered over the keys as I decided what I wanted to say.

33

CAMILA

*A*s darkness settled over the city, Aunt Brianna and I sat in front of my gas fireplace. Kit Kat was curled up in front of it on her little rug, fast asleep.

I'd always thought the flames looked real, but after spending a couple of days in the cabin with Beau in front of a REAL fire, I couldn't help noticing that my fireplace was fake.

It was too bad, because the flames were real. Gas flames. But the logs were not. The logs never burned up. And they had very little scent. I had a holiday candle burning over the fireplace to add a bit of spruce tree scent, but it wasn't the same.

And somehow that bothered me.

"It's a lovely fire," Aunt Brianna said. Aunt Brianna didn't look a day over thirty. It was hard to believe that she had children of her own.

And she always, including right now, looked like she stepped out of the pages of a magazine.

Made sense since she had her own You Tube Channel with about a billion followers.

"Thanks," I said with a forced smile.

Something was wrong with my head.

It was a lovely fire.

But I kept thinking about the fire in the cabin. The REAL fire.

It wasn't the fire so much, though, that I was thinking about. It was Beau.

And seeing him today…

"What's bothering you?" Aunt Brianna asked, swirling the cabernet in her glass.

Aunt Brianna might not be a psychologist, but she cut to the chase. Or maybe she cut to the chase because she wasn't a psychologist.

I sat back, swirled my own wine. Took a sip.

"I don't know how to tell you," I said. Aunt Brianna was so composed. Her life was so together. She and Uncle Jackson had such a good life.

Mine felt so… messy… in comparison.

I should just marry Todd and be done with it. I shouldn't be thinking about breaking up with him to be with someone else. Someone no one knew. I would be an embarrassment to the family.

"This has something to do with Todd?" Aunt Brianna asked, taking a sip of her wine.

My gaze shot to hers. "How do you…?"

Aunt Brianna smiled. "I just have a gut feeling about these things."

"Todd hasn't done anything wrong," I said, closing my eyes for a minute.

"I have to confess how I know. Ainsley saw you at the hospital."

"Oh," I said, sitting back and staring at Aunt Brianna. She didn't seem the least bit surprised, much less upset.

"Look," Aunt Brianna said. "I haven't said anything because it's not my business, but I've noticed that you and Todd don't really have... appear to have... much of a spark." She held up a hand. "I could be wrong. Not my place."

I blew out a breath. I don't know if I was shocked or relieved. Maybe both.

"But Todd's sort of part of the family."

"Honey," Aunt Brianna said. "Todd is only part of the family if you want him to be."

"What do you mean?"

"It's simple." She put a hand on my arm. "You and me are family. Jackson is family because I want him to be. If you want Todd, we'll all love him. If you want someone else, we'll love him just as much."

"It sounds so easy," I said.

"Because it is."

"So..." she said with a little mischievous grin. "tell me about the mystery guy."

Why not? I had asked Aunt Brianna to come over here. I at least owed her an explanation.

"He's the guy from the cabin. The one who rescued me."

"You found him?"

"Not exactly?" Kit Kat jumped into my lap and nudged my hand onto her head.

"He found you?"

I shook my head. "Sophia. Beau was one of the paramedics who came."

"Oh. My. God." Aunt Brianna set her glass down. "It's Kismet."

"I don't know," I said. I had thought about it, but I think I was afraid to believe it. "I think it's just a coincidence."

"But you like him?"

I tried not to smile. It happened anyway.

"You do," she said.

"I do like him, but… he didn't get my phone number and I don't have his. I don't even know his last name."

Aunt Brianna rolled her eyes. "It's not like you're all that hard to find."

34

BEAU

I walked into the unit office the next morning and stowed my things in my locker.

It was always quiet here. Somber even.

I wanted to start my shift. Get to work and avoid seeing anyone.

But when I turned around, I nearly bumped right into Lucy.

"Hi," she said. "Feeling better?"

"Yes, thank you."

I kept walking, hoping to avoid an uncomfortable conversation.

I'd simply told Lucy I would see her in the morning. No explanation.

I'd weighed it out. I didn't want to do anything to lead Lucy on. Not when I was already more than smitten by someone else.

It didn't matter that I didn't know what I was going to do about it yet. I did know that I was going to do something.

"Maybe tonight?" she asked as I walked off.

"Maybe," I said over my shoulder. But definitely not.

I'd obviously given Lucy the wrong impression. Either that or she didn't bother to ask if I was available. That bothered me a bit about her. I hadn't told anyone here that I was single. Or not. She had just assumed.

Or maybe she didn't care. There were a ton of those women out there.

And that was exactly what bothered me about Camila. I didn't want to be the guy trying to break up something that she and Todd had.

She'd said she didn't want to marry him.

I could argue with myself all day. But the outcome was the same.

I wanted her to be happy.

And if that meant giving her up, then so be it. Sometimes loving someone meant letting them go.

"Beau." It was my boss. "You've got a phone call."

"Me?" Why was someone calling me here?

How was someone calling me here?

No one knew where I was.

I walked into my boss's office and picked up the phone.

"Beau." I didn't recognize the male voice. "This is Edward, your mother's husband."

I had not seen my mother for a good ten years, but it didn't keep the fear from striking deep in my heart.

"What's wrong?" I asked.

"Your mother is in the hospital," he said. "She's asking for you."

"What happened?" I pressed my fingertips against the bridge of my nose and closed my eyes. I needed to take a breath.

"There was an accident," he said. "Can you come?"

"Where?"

"Venice."

Venice. Halfway across the world.

"How serious is it?" I asked, knowing it didn't really matter. She was my mother.

"She's in surgery now. I just thought you might want to know. To be here for her."

"Of course," I said. Of course I did.

I had met Edward once. He seemed like a decent guy. At the time I had just been pissed at the world, and him especially since he was marrying my mother. I didn't understand how she could be getting married again.

"Text the details to my phone," I said. "And I'll see what I can do."

"It's already arranged," he said. "You have a flight booked already."

I set the phone down and stood looked out the window at the traffic on the freeway.

This was not how I had intended for my day to go.

But it had to be done.

I found my supervisor, tossing supplies for the day into his bag. "I have to go to Venice," I said.

"Okay. When?"

"Now." My mind was racing with all the things I had to do. "Something came up."

I was being vague on purpose. I was always vague. The less people knew, I figured, the less they would have to use against me. Not sure where I picked that up, but it had sunk in deep.

"Sorry to leave you like this," I said. "But it's a family matter."

"Understood," Mark said. Mark was a good man. Very understanding.

"I'll let you know when I'm on my way back," I said.

Any plans I had for today, tomorrow, the rest of the week had just vanished into nothing.

I'd wanted time to think. I was just about to get a lot of time to think on an airplane ride across the ocean.

There was one good thing about it. I didn't have to face Lucy for awhile.

35

CAMILA

I sat in the cockpit of a sweet little Cessna. My heart was pounding like it had on my very first solo flight back in the day.

My clearance to fly again had come out of the blue a week before Christmas.

I considered it an early Christmas present. Probably less to do with Santa than with Grandpa Noah. He practically ran the aviation industry.

A beautiful Texas December day. Blue clouds. Warm. Seventy degrees. No wind.

It had been a week and one day since Sophia's accident on the ice… the same day I had spent with Beau.

I checked the computer screens. Everything seemed to be in order.

I shouldn't be nervous.

The results from my crash had come back. It had been a system failure. Nothing I could have done. Nothing that could have been prevented. A once in a million occurrence.

I was a good pilot. I could do this.

I had no particular destination in mind. Just going up. Taking the plane for a spin. Come back down.

Tomorrow I would go back to work. Take a passenger to Dallas.

The roar of the motor settled my nerves as I took off, left the ground.

My favorite part of flying. When the plane first took off, air beneath the wings.

I went up, headed toward downtown. I liked flying around the city. Loved the skyline. If I had super powerful vision, I could see the Rocky Mountains from here.

I couldn't, of course. That was just wishful thinking. Maybe I should have headed in that direction.

Really get back on the horse. Thankfully I wasn't debilitatingly nervous about flying again. Not remembering anything about the crash probably helped.

I honestly think that if I could have skipped the whole therapy thing and got right back in the air, I would have been better off. The way they had it set up, I had far too much time to think about it.

I'd thought about Beau some, too. Some. I thought about him all the time.

I had not, however, talked to Todd yet. Our schedules just hadn't matched. He had been doing a lot of extra flying this month with the holidays and all.

I looked down, saw the festive decorations—the trees and all—along Post Oak. Now that it was colder, down in the forties, it seemed more like Christmas.

But it all just made me sad. I hadn't heard from Beau.

Aunt Brianna assured me that Beau would know how to find me. She told me not to worry, but it was easy for her to say.

I should not have told Beau about Todd.

He could so easily have gotten the wrong impression. He

probably thought I actually *wanted* to marry Todd even though I said I didn't. Why else would I have stayed with him?

Whatever. Todd and I were meeting tonight. Having dinner. And I was going to break up with him.

I had decided. I was not going to go through another Christmas with someone I wasn't in love with.

Feeling better, I squared my shoulders. After tonight I would be free of Todd. Officially.

I circled around and headed back to the airport. I wanted to get home and changed into a dress. I wanted to look my best tonight. Was that a little bit wrong? Human nature, I guess. I wanted him to know what he was losing.

Getting a good view of the airport, I spoke into my headset. Got permission to land.

Just as my wheels hit the ground, I got a text from Todd. He was back at the airport early. He had in fact, just landed.

I fought a knee-jerk reflex to abort my landing and come back later. But that was just silly. I had no reason to actively avoid Todd. Maybe I could admit to sort of avoiding him a little bit while I knew I needed to break up with him.

As I taxied toward the terminal, I saw his plane sitting on the tarmac, the red Skye Travels logo splashed across the tail of his Lear jet. He had literally just landed, too. Very unusual for us to randomly end up at the airport at the same time.

I made a smooth landing and taxied along the runway, reaching the private terminal and starting the process of securing the aircraft.

The door to Todd's plane opened up and he lowered the stairs. He really had just landed.

A man and a woman stepped out, followed shortly by Todd.

I was struck anew how handsome Todd was. He looked good in his uniform. I shook my head. No matter what happened with Beau, I knew now that Todd was not the man for me. Handsome or not.

The passengers had to walk past my plane to get to the Skye Travels terminal.

I mostly ignored them as I went down my post-flight checklist.

But I happened to glance up just as they walked past.

I froze.

No.

It was Beau.

Beau?

What the—?

Then I noticed the woman walking alongside him.

Shoulder-length long hair. Dark shades over her eyes.

But she was tall and had on spiky high heels. As they walked together, she kept her hand in the crook of his arm.

They seemed… familiar with each other. Comfortable. He leaned over. Said something. She laughed. Leaned her cheek on his arm.

I watched until they were inside the terminal. Then I just sat there.

I felt numb.

That explained everything.

Beau hadn't tracked me down because he was with someone. A wife at the most. A girlfriend at the least.

"Camila?" Someone was tapping on the window. I looked down. Saw one of the techs.

I couldn't just sit here forever.

I had to keep moving.

My heart was breaking like a sheet of ice. A small rock had hit me in the center and the ice was shattering into a thousand pieces.

That's how it went, it seemed. Someone broke my heart and I was about to go break someone else's.

36

BEAU

"*I*t's nice to spend time with you," Mom said.

"I agree," I said, handing her a cup of steaming hot cocoa.

We sat in my apartment on the twenty-fourth floor. It was just a little one bedroom, but it was perfect for me. And best of all, it had a fireplace, even if it did have gas flames.

"I'm sorry it had to be so long since we've seen other," she said. "and under such circumstances."

"You don't have to apologize." I sat on the couch next to her. I'd be sleeping here later, giving her my bed.

I had a couch and a bed. That's it. Enough furniture for any single man in my book.

"Yes. I do. I'm the mother."

"We're both at fault," I said. "I'm just glad you're okay." When Mom's husband had called to tell me she had been in an accident, it had been a little bit of an overreaction. She had injured her spleen and was healing nicely. I was glad he had called me, though, when he did.

"Me too."

"And you have a great husband. It was nice of him to let you come a couple of days early so we could have some time."

"Beau," she said, looking at me over the rim of her mug. "I'm so proud of the man you've turned out to be."

I didn't say anything. It was odd having her say these things. She hadn't seen me since I left for the Air Force. To her I guess I looked like I had things together. To me, I felt like I still had a long way to go.

"This is a wonderful view," she said, looking out over the city lights spread out below. "But why Houston? We never lived here."

"Maybe that's why," I said, with a little grin.

She looked at me sideways. "That doesn't sound like you."

"Why do you say that?"

She was staring out over the city. "I never told you this, but I overheard you talking to your father one time. Before that last time…"

She took a deep breath. Kept going. "The two of you were talking about how nice it would be to settle down. Maybe get a cabin in the mountains."

"I don't remember that," I said. But the whole cabin in the woods thing had come from somewhere. I'd never given much thought to where exactly I had acquired that affinity.

"So I'm thinking maybe there was another reason."

She was awfully perceptive to not have seen me and barely talked to me for the last ten years of my adult life.

"There might be a girl," I said.

"There is a God," she said, setting her mug aside.

I rolled my eyes at her.

"When do I get to meet her?"

"I don't know."

"You're protecting her from your mother?" she asked, teasingly bumping a shoulder against him.

"Actually," I said. "I don't even have her phone number yet."

Now she was just looking at me. It reminded me of how she looked at me after I'd claimed to have done my homework when she knew perfectly well I had not.

"Well," she said. "How do you plan to get it?"

"I'm not sure," I said. "but I have a couple of ideas."

"Don't let me stand in your way Beau Montrose," she said.

I laughed.

Family. That was one thing I had been missing from my life.

And having my mother back in my life was like a special gift for the holidays.

It was nice to have someone around who was in my corner.

37

CAMILA

*C*hristmas Eve. The Houston Galleria was alive with the holiday spirit.

Carolers were caroling. Birds were singing. Actually a bird had gotten inside the mall and had made a nest near the top of the tree Christmas tree. She was spotted flying around on occasion.

A noisy crowd had gathered around the skating rink. The bottom floor, the second floor, and the third floor in anticipation of the Houston Figure Skating Christmas Extravaganza.

Sophia was billed as the highlight of the show.

Wearing a long winter white wool coat, I sat on the ground floor, between Aunt Ainsley and Aunt Brianna. Two sets of benches had been brought in for the occasion. Most people stood, though.

The music was loud, but only occasional snatches could be heard over the excited voices of all ages.

The rest of the family was here, including Grandpa Noah and Grandma Savannah, but my two favorite aunts kept me close.

I took a sip of the hot peppermint mocha coffee that I held in my warm cashmere gloves.

It had been a week—nearly—since I had broken up with Todd. He had taken it better than I had expected. I think he had been expecting it.

The fact that he had taken it without an ounce of drama confirmed in my mind that we had very little passion for each other.

My family, surprisingly, had taken it in stride. And though they didn't say it in so many words, they thought the sadness that had settled over me was because of Todd.

I didn't correct them. I just didn't say much of anything.

Since I was working again, I wasn't always available, but on those mornings when I brought Sophia to the skating rink for her practice, I couldn't help but look for Beau. It was silly, of course.

He was taken. I gave up on shoving him out of my mind and just dealt with the sadness.

The conversation hushed, making the music louder.

Everyone's attention was on the front entrance of the skating rink.

Four girls wearing red skating dresses glided out first, in perfect formation. Then four more wearing green skating dresses. Then four more wearing red.

And just like that, the ice rink was filled with a swirl of red and green coordinated motion.

The girls, from six to eight year old, were all very talented and lovely on the ice.

Then Sophia skated out. She was wearing a sparkling blue skating dress and blue skates that I had helped her pick out.

As she skated toward the Christmas tree, the other girls skated around her in what I knew was the result of hours of practice.

Sophia came around the tree, went into a series of step

sequences, some pirouettes that dazzled the audience. I held my breath each time, but she was amazing.

Then she disappeared into the fold of the other skaters, coming out with a perfectly executed stunning axel jump.

She came to a stop. All the skaters did. And they bowed with grace and elegance.

They had just pulled off a show worthy of any age group.

Then the rink was flooded with a cascade of long stem roses in reds and whites, from a net across the ceiling.

One particular flower, a white rose, floated more slowly than the others. It fell delicately like a leaf in the wind.

It floated right down to Sophia. Not the least bit surprised, she took it in her hands and skated toward us.

I looked at Aunt Brianna, thinking Sophia was doing something special for her mother.

But instead, she held it out to me.

"For you, Aunt Camila," she whispered.

"What?"

I took the rose from her and just held it, looking blankly at her.

"It has a message," she said.

My fingers shaking, I carefully unrolled the paper wrapped around the stem.

Sophia turned and skated back, leading the other twelve girls off the ice. She looked like a princess, her ladies trailing behind her.

I opened the note and read.

Will you be my forever Christmas Angel?

My heart raced, sending the blood racing through my veins.

Christmas *Angel?*

I looked over at Aunt Brianna. She just smiled and shrugged.

I pressed the rose to my cheek, not sure what to make of it. Read the note again.

Since we had to wait for Sophia, we stayed seated.

With the show over, the crowd began to disperse. At first I didn't notice the man standing on the other side of the skating rink. I'm sure he had been there all along, just a man in a charcoal suit, blending in with everyone else in the crowd.

Then I saw him. Really saw him.

Beau?

He looked so different in the suit. I'd only seen him in jeans and a flannel shirt or scrubs.

When he grinned, I knew for sure it was him.

Without thinking, I stood up and started moving away from the bleachers.

Before stepping out into the crowded walkway, I looked back, but he was gone.

I had the sinking feeling that I had imagined him after all.

But the flower and the note in my hands suggested otherwise.

I had not imagined them.

The area around the skating rink was so crowded. The mall was about to close and with the show over, everyone was moving about.

I ducked between people, making slow progress around the rink. I looked everywhere.

I reached the other side of the skating rink and looked toward where he had been standing.

But he wasn't there.

I had imagined him then.

"Hello Angel."

I whirled at the sound of his voice behind me.

He stood there looking at me.

Then I was in his arms and the rest of the world faded as I pressed my cheek against his chest.

"I want you to meet someone," he said, pulling back to look into my eyes.

"Okay."

"My mother and stepfather are here."

His mother. Of course. That's who I had seen him with at the airport.

"I missed you Camila," he said. "But you had Todd and I didn't want to be the one who came between you."

I was shaking my head. I lifted the rose. "How did you...?"

"I had a little help from a six-year-old."

"Sophia."

"And maybe your Aunt Brianna."

It was just like Aunt Brianna to be involved in something like this.

"We have an audience," he said.

I turned and saw who had to be his mother and stepfather. Aunt Brianna. Sophia. Aunt Ainsley.

"Do you care?" he asked.

"Do I care what?"

"Do you care if they see me kiss you?"

"I don't care who sees," I said.

And then his lips were on mine and world settled beneath my feet.

EPILOGUE

Nine Months Later

"Your family must think there's something wrong with us," Beau said, popping a cube of Havarti in his mouth and leaning back on his elbows.

Although we had a brand new sofa, compliments of Beau Montrose, the new owner, we sat on a soft pallet on the floor.

The fire cast the only light in the cabin. The REAL fire that burned real wood. There were stacks of it. Some of it was left over from last year. Some of it was newly chopped.

"Why do you say that?" I asked, swirling the cabernet in my glass.

"Because we could go anyplace we wanted for our honeymoon." He swept a hand vaguely around the little cabin with the one little bed. "And we came here."

"There's nothing wrong with here," I said. "Besides, they understand."

"They will probably hate me forever for bringing you here instead of some exotic place like Paris."

"Bah," I said "We can go to Paris anytime. Besides…" I set my wine glass aside. "Here I have your full attention."

"You have my full attention anywhere," he said, kissing me on the tip of my nose. "Everywhere."

"So you say," I said.

"Actually," he said, glancing at his watch. "I do have a surprise for you."

"Wait," I said, taking his arm. "What is this?"

"What? My watch?"

"Yes." I unbuckled his Apple watch and set it aside. "Time is supposed to stand still on one's honeymoon."

"Okay," he said. "But your surprise is supposed to be here at five-fifteen."

"What surprise?" I picked up his watch. It was almost five.

"If I tell you, it won't be a surprise."

"What do we have to do?" I asked. "Turn on the radio or something?"

He laughed, taking his watch back and setting it aside. "You have made a good point. We don't have to do anything."

I looked at him suspiciously. He was acting funny. We had arrived in Whiskey Springs last night and hiked out to the cabin this morning. He hadn't said anything about any kind of surprise.

"Well then." I sat up straighter. Beau gave good surprises.

Then I heard some rustling on the front porch.

"Something's out there," I whispered, trying to remember if we had locked the door.

"He's early," Beau said, getting up.

"Who's early?"

"Your surprise," he said with a grin.

I was shaking my head. I did not want company. I only wanted to be alone with Beau.

But he opened the door anyway.

Before I could even stand up, there was a blurry bundle of black fur heading toward me.

I shrieked and covered my head.

"Biscuit," Beau said. "Sit."

"Biscuit?"

The dog sat.

Beau closed the door and came to sit back down on our little pallet.

I put my arms down and looked at the dog.

"Biscuit?"

Biscuit looked at Beau.

"Go ahead," he said.

Then Biscuit was licking my face and I was rubbing his fur.

"How?" I looked toward the door. "Who?"

"I had him delivered."

"Delivered by who?"

"You ask a lot of questions, Mrs. Montrose."

I was not deterred. "So he's visiting?"

Beau handed me a little box.

"What's this?"

"Open it," he said.

It was a dog collar. I looked at the tag. *Biscuit* was engraved on the front. *Camila Montrose* and my phone number engraved on the back.

I dropped the collar in my lap. "I truly don't understand."

"He's a companion for Kit Kat."

I looked blankly at him.

"He's yours, Love." He sat down next to me and gathered me in his arms.

"How?" I asked, my eyes moist with unshed tears. Happy tears.

"I'll explain everything later," he said.

Biscuit barked one time, then going to his place in front of the fire, turned around three times and laid down.

"I think that's our cue," Beau said.

And then he kissed me.

We had come full circle. I'd had to lose my past to find my future.

I'd found Beau. My forever.

And now, somehow, we had a dog named Biscuit.

Beau Montrose had a lot of explaining to do.

But that would most certainly wait until after the best part of the honeymoon.

Keep Reading for a Preview of Begin Again...

BEGIN AGAIN PREVIEW

*S*avannah Richards didn't believe in chance.

But there he stood, head bent, focused on his iPad. Handsome in his black uniform - black tie, white shirt, silver stripes at his wrists. A captain's cap sitting atop his head His hair graying around the edges.

Noah wouldn't recognize her now – even if he remembered her.

He would be forty-two now. A far cry from the college senior who had been attached to her hip for a year. He'd been a boy then, but his features were the same. A few pounds heavier, but that was to be expected. The five o'clock shadow that never failed to appear by early afternoon. The same brow that she had seen furrowed over a calculous problem seemed to have made a permanent home between his eyes. No wonder, as he had worn it often. Sometimes even as he'd studied her, though he thought she hadn't known.

As a college senior, the only time he'd left her side was when he was flying or training to fly. Sometimes she'd gone with him to practice on the simulator. She usually ended up using the time to study her own biology textbooks or read an English lit novel. Side by side, each lost in their own world.

The time, she thought wryly, had been well spent. After her freshman year, Savannah had immersed herself in her studies and graduated top of her class with a bachelor's degree in science.

Noah also had displayed a singular passion – aviation. And everything that went with it. Flying. Airplanes. Weather reports. When he hadn't been engrossed in aviation, however, he'd turned that singular focus on her. The memory brought a flush to her cheeks.

And a familiar stab to her heart.

As the terminal train arrived at the station and the door opened to allow people to exit, it occurred to her that she could take six steps to the left, get in his train car, and speak to him. It was a much more logical thing to do than just watching him – letting him breeze by her.

Two ships passing in the night.

No. He was a ship from the past. She would let him go.

She was still mad at him.

NOAH WORTHINGTON GLARED at the flight schedule displayed on his iPad and wondered if his lunch had not agreed with him. The terminal train at Atlanta airport was interminably slow. He wasn't sure if he wanted it to hurry up or to never arrive. He struggled to find a middle ground.

He was seeing an apparition. He knew it had to be a vision because the girl he recognized wore a snug red pencil skirt with matching suit jacket. Her black pumps, though, had a matching red bottom. She carried a black leather Louis Vuitton handbag in a cross-body style, freeing up her hands. He recognized the LV twist-lock on the front – its only readily identifiable feature. The silver on the handbag matched the buttons on her suit. And the gray of her camisole. Her long brunette hair fell in loose waves around her face. Her make-up was flawless down to the shiny, but muted glossy red lipstick.

The college freshman from his indelible memory wore jeans ripped at the knees, white canvas sneakers, and either a sweatshirt or t-shirt depending on the weather. She'd kept her hair pulled back in a loose ponytail. The only time he'd seen her dressed up was when she wore a dark gray cardigan and matching shell with black slacks to a dinner with his family. She'd worn low heeled dark gray moto boots. He'd been impressed, at the time, at how put together and cute she looked. Her hair had fallen straight to her shoulder and though he hadn't commented, he'd known she had taken the time to straighten it with a flat iron. Her hair was naturally wavy and thick and she hated it. Hence, the ponytail.

All in all, perhaps that was a precursor to the woman who watched him now. Or perhaps she was his mind's rendition of the girlfriend he'd so inconsiderately left behind twenty years ago. Besides, what college freshman gained no more than a couple of pounds and in all the right places after twenty years?

The vision watched him, though she didn't know he knew. He recognized the expression she wore.

She was still mad at him.

The train rolled in, the door opened, and throngs of people rushed out of the cars. She got into the car behind his, moving with that same lilt in her step that even he hadn't managed to dull.

She's only a vision. Probably some random girl from California who just happened to have similar – very similar facial features.

However, he knew the saying that one never forgot his first love to be true.

He glanced at the time on his tablet. He had time for dinner before his flight, now delayed, took off for Dallas. He didn't feel like going to the officer's club. Didn't feel like talking aviation. Or hearing about someone's new aircraft acquisition. He just wanted to enjoy some peaceful time to read his novel, order a martini he wouldn't drink, and have a meal.

He scanned his ID and slipped into the Diner's Club – away from the other pilots. He wasn't exactly nondescript in his pilot's uniform, but he'd learned over the years that the typical flyer tended to not bother the pilots. He'd never quite discerned if it was out of respect, awe, or fear. Perhaps just disinterest. Whatever it was, he'd grown to count on it when he wanted to be left alone.

He took a small table for two near the bar, his back to the room. He found it less distracting to read when he couldn't see people hurrying to and fro.

He ordered a sandwich and water. And resumed his attention on the novel he read on his iPad. It was about a man who never slept. In theory, he liked the concept, but in reality, sleep was one of his favorite pastimes.

And allowed the world to fade into the background. Which was exactly where he preferred it these days.

"I'd like a cosmopolitan," A woman at the bar behind him ordered. "with olives."

Who ordered olives with their cosmopolitans?

The server said something he couldn't understand. And the woman laughed.

Noah froze. Then in slow motion lifted his head and turned enough to see the woman in the red suit.

She had not been a vision. She was Savannah Skye Richards. His college sweetheart all grown up.

He'd recognized her, but his mind had refused to accept the reality that after twenty years, she'd be standing in front of him.

Closing his iPad, he laid it on the table and silently turned his chair around so he could watch her. He leaned back, his six-foot frame appearing relaxed – disguising the cat-like tension coursing through him.

She hadn't spotted him yet. Her gaze was glued to her phone – her fingers typing rapidly. The years had been good to her. She'd always been pretty, but now... she was drop-dead gorgeous. There was an air about her that hadn't been there when she was struggling in college. She carried an air of assurance and confidence now that hadn't been there before.

Twenty years. Then twice random crossings in less than an hour. It was more than he could ignore.

She must have felt him watching her. She glanced up, typed a couple of key-strokes. Then looked up again. He could tell by the way the corners of her mouth twitched the moment his presence registered with her. With her new self-assurance, he was certain that only he could tell. He'd spent, after all, countless hours studying her. For nearly a whole year.

Their gazes locked. He smiled. God, but it was good to see her.

Déjà vu was an understatement.

He'd been working registration his senior year. She was a freshman. Her first day on campus at Auburn University in Auburn, Alabama. He'd taken one look at her and fallen head over heels.

This time, however, instead of smiling, she was looking... displeased to see him.

He stood up, closed the distance between them, and sat at the bar next to her. "What brings you to this gin joint?" he said.

"Work," she said, clicking off her iPhone.

"It's been awhile," he said.

"Twenty years," she said, as the server set her cosmopolitan in front of her. She picked it up. Sipped.

"What are the odds?" he asked.

"I don't believe in chance." She kept her eyes focused on her drink.

"I guess a date at the casino is out."

She scoffed. "A date is out."

"Savannah Skye," he said.

"Savannah," she corrected.

He rubbed his chin. "Savannah. Look at me," She lifted her eyes and he saw a glimpse of the pain before she checked it.

"It's been twenty years since we saw each other. Let's at least say hello."

"Hello," she said.

"That's better."

She scowled again. "You started it."

He shook his head. "You're right. I did. I'm sorry. I was caught off guard."

She smiled, albeit a little wobbly. "I'm sorry, too. I've seen you twice in one day. That can't be coincidence."

"I agree," he said. "You look good. You look like I imagined."

She raised an eyebrow. "You imagined me."

He chuckled. "On occasion, yes."

"You're married," she pointed out, nodding toward his ring finger.

He glanced down. Saw the line on his ring finger, no more than a shadow to most. She always had been observant. "Divorced. Separated actually."

"Right," she said, looking at him askance. "Aren't you all?"

"What?"

She shrugged.

"It seems you've been hanging around the wrong crowd."

"Is that so? When's your divorce hearing date?"

"I don't know."

She rolled her eyes. Sipped her drink.

"Seriously. It's uncontested. I'm not even sure we have to go."

She glanced at him. Unlocked her phone.

"Ok. Here," he said, taking his own phone out of his pocket. "Let's call Matthew. Let's call my attorney."

"Let's don't."

"Why are you so interested in my marital state?"

"Ok, let's say for now I believe you."

"No, really, why are you?"

Her gaze met his now. She chuckled. "You've already asked me out."

"I most certainly did not."

"The casino," she said, locking her phone again.

He shook his head, "It's a figure of speech. When did you become so literal?"

She leaned back. Sighed. "After being hit on about five hundred times."

"Admirable," he said, "I can see the attraction."

She laughed. "Not like that. As part of my job."

He considered her in a different light now. Her clothes were much too fine for a stripper. Definitely not a prostitute.

"You're an escort?"

She sighed. "I see you never developed a filter."

He shrugged. "Some things never change."

"I'm not a call girl." She glared at him. "Or a prostitute. So don't get any ideas."

"I think you're about twenty-one years late on that request."

"Yeah, well, you're married now."

"Separated."

"Same thing."

"You're difficult. I'm impressed. What about you?"

He'd yet to get a glimpse of her ring finger. Truthfully, he'd been too enthralled to even think to look.

She held up her unadorned hand.

"Divorced?"

"Never married."

"Are you telling me that you never..." He trailed off. This conversation was completely unfair. He had no way to know what damage he'd done to her all those years ago.

"I work a lot."

He nodded. Self-sufficient. Successful. Hence the air of confidence. "What kind of work?"

"I'm a drug rep."

"Really?" Not at all what he expected.

"You may recall I was a science major."

"I do recall. And I'm sure you excelled."

"You could say that."

He smiled to himself. She had that slightly pouty expression that had always worked on him.

"I'm a pilot," he said, before he could stop himself.

She laughed. A genuine laugh now. Her green eyes twinkled with sincerity.

And it was in that moment. Just like that, that the years fell away and he was that college senior all over again. In love with the freshman coed.

"I never would have guessed."

"Did the uniform give me away?"

"That and the unerring devotion you put toward achieving that goal."

He sat a little taller in his chair. "You're successful at this drug rep thing you do," he said.

She tilted her head with a little smile. "I suppose. Why would you say that?"

"Because you're good at everything you do and..." he lifted one eyebrow suggestively. "You have a way of making a man do whatever it is you want."

She shook her head. The smile disappeared back into the little pout. "That seems a little odd coming from you." A silent message appeared on her phone. She checked it and pushed her unfinished drink aside.

"I'm sorry," she said.

She had managed to do it again. She had mesmerized him and he had no idea what she was talking about. "Sorry about what?"

"I have to go."

"Go?" He checked his watch. Such a short time had passed since he'd come into the club… yet his life, it seemed, had been altered forever.

The girl he had spent twenty years wondering about. Twenty years with a love in his heart that hadn't died.

And here she was. In the flesh.

"Yes," she said, with the flash of a smile at the corner of her lips. "I have a flight to catch." She stood up.

"Of course you do." *Why else would she be here?* For a mere moment in time, he'd allowed himself to think that she was there in his world just for him. Just for him and no one else.

She stood up. Pushed her chair to the bar. "It was good to see you again, Noah," she said, her lips curved in a polite smile no doubt used successfully when working with doctors.

"It was good to see you, too," he said, automatically.

She held out her hand.

He took her hand, but didn't shake it as she had obviously intended, but held it. Stared into those mesmerizing green eyes. She pulled back almost imperceptibly. He held tighter. Felt a gut-wrenching juxtaposition of familiar and new as she gave in and squeezed back. Just for a moment.

A moment in time. When his heart was light and the world narrowed down to them. Just the two of them.

"I'm gonna miss my flight," she said, pulling back in earnest now.

He released her. "Go," he said.

She picked up her bag and turned. Took a step.

His heart sank. Heavy again.

"Wait," he said, out of his chair in a flash and closing the distance between them. Stepping in front of her.

She raised an eyebrow.

"How will I find you?"

Her lips curved into a smug little smile. The smile he'd seen her wear after she aced a chemistry exam. "Perhaps we'll bump into each other again," she said.

"No," he insisted. "It's been twenty years. We both travel all the time. Right? You travel?"

"A fair amount."

"Well, you don't believe in chance. Yet in one day, we've bumped into each other twice… in one hour."

She shrugged. "What are the odds?"

He scoffed. "Out of the mouth of the one who doesn't believe in chance."

"I believe in science."

"Well, scientifically, we could never see each other again."

"You could always look for me this time."

He absorbed the jab. Owned it. "I could. I will. But the world is a big place."

She seemed to consider. Squinted into his eyes. Searching for something only she knew to look for.

"New York."

"New York what?"

"I'll be in New York for the next five days."

"Ha. New York doesn't narrow the world by very much."

She nodded. "It is a big city. But you know enough about me to find me."

"Wait," he said. "Until Monday?"

"Tuesday."

"Come on," he said. She turned. Smiled over her shoulder. That smile that had once been reserved only for him.

"See you around," she said, and walked away from him. He watched her walk through the door.

Keep Reading BEGIN AGAIN...

Kathryn Kaleigh is the author of over seventy novels, over one hundred short stories, and many collections.

kathrynkaleigh.com